Ruth Hay writes women's fiction
for discerning readers.
Discover her Prime Time and Seafarer books
today!

Prime Time Series
Auld Acquaintance
Time Out of Mind
Now or Never
Sand in the Wind
With This Ring
The Seas Between Us

Seafarers Series
Sea Changes
Sea Tides

It is better to ask some of the questions than to know all the answers.

James Thurber.

One.

Zoe Morton arrived early at her office, primed and ready for the day.

She relished the quiet of the building and the sense of pride she always felt at what she had accomplished there. It had been a long, hard climb to Chief Executive Officer and she took not one step of it for granted. Best of all, she knew she had made it on her own. There was no powerful husband behind her, although there had been a few useful male friendships along the way to boost her position.

Her seat in the boardroom of Excelsior Pharmaceuticals had been secured through her ability to innovate, recognize talent, budget appropriately and keep a good team around her. When others fell by the wayside, Zoe Morton forged on, distinguished by her classic clothing style, always in black and white, her no nonsense meetings, and her exemplary work ethic.

Suzanne met her with a smile and a china cup of Arabica coffee brewed specially for her each morning.

"Good morning, Miss Morton, the mail is on your desk. Three invitations to speak at conferences and one personal letter, unopened of course. I have vetted the overnight emails and left the relevant ones on your laptop. The day's schedule has one change of time for your meeting with Research and Development and a quick meeting at noon about a new request for anti-malarial vaccine funding."

"Thank you, Suzanne. Give me fifteen minutes to enjoy my coffee and finish the company announcements then we'll tackle the rest of the day."

"Certainly, Miss Morton."

Suzanne softly closed the door to the executive suite. She knew well her boss' likes and dislikes. These few minutes at the start of her day were sacrosanct and also gave her secretary a chance to take the temperature of the day from their brief exchange.

Brand new suit in a subdued check with a favourite white blouse peeking out. That bodes well.

A little tiredness around the eyes, but it's a very hectic time of year.

Not too much mail today, so a clear start. Just that one unusual letter. I hope I was right to include it. Working on pure instinct there. Should be a good day and perhaps I can get her out a little earlier. The weather report promises a fine afternoon.

Zoe sipped her coffee and flipped through the emails quickly. She picked up the stiff cards, easily identified by their stamped logos, and rejected two of the invitations. She had already decided to attend the medical conference in the Midlands, as keynote speaker.

The personal letter was unusual. Nothing on the envelope conveyed the source. Normally, Suzanne would deal with anything like this. She knew her boss had no time for begging letters or time-wasters of that kind.

The address was hand-written. Who did that these days?

She turned the envelope over and immediately saw the letters printed on the flap.

S.W.A.L.K. Sealed With A Loving Kiss.

Her eyes teared up and her breath stopped for a moment. Only one person had ever used this style of address on her letters and that person, her mother, was dead.

She was thrown back years to the day of the funeral; undoubtedly one of the worst days of her life.

As if to match her mood of abject despair, the rain had poured down and even the parson had rushed to get the graveside service over. By the end, only Zoe and her mother's best friends were left, arm in arm for support. If Valerie and Sandra had not held tight to her, she knew she would have sunk to her knees in the mud and perhaps never risen again.

Shaken to the core, Zoe turned away from her desk and looked out at the sky view while she breathed deeply and tried to stop her hands from trembling. Who had done this to her? Who had known about her mother's private sign?

There was no way to avoid it. She ripped open the envelope and began to read.

My dear Zoe,
I know it has been too long since we have been in touch but, as you probably heard, things have been difficult here.
I have been thinking about you and Grace lately and I want you to seriously consider what I am about to ask.
I have rented a spacious apartment in Ambleside for one week next month and I am inviting your mother's best friends to join me

there.

It is high time to renew our bonds with each other. Life is short and the water rises, as I know to be true.

I can promise a beautiful location, good food and lots of interesting places to see in the area. Good conversation is guaranteed.

Please don't say you are too busy. For your own sake, and in your mother's memory, I beg you to join us.

It's only a few days out of your life, but I know they will be significant.

Aunt Valerie.

Her first impulse was to throw the letter away. How dare she?

Valerie Westwood was not a real aunt. It was an honorary title bestowed by her mother on the close group of friends. How rude of her to presume a CEO could just drop everything and rush off to the Lake District on a whim. It had been two years since she had taken more than a weekend off. If she were to take a vacation it would not be with an old pal of her mother's generation. What benefit would there be in that? The anger that now swept through her, banished the shakes. She was Zoe Morton. She was not at the beck and call of just anyone, even someone who had been important to her mother. No chance of that.

Yes, she had seen the obituary some months ago when David Westwood had died. Suzanne had copied it for her from the newspaper since she was responsible for collating any references to her boss' name or company. Her mother's name had been included in the obituary as 'Grace Morton, late, much-beloved friend of Valerie and David Westwood'.

Zoe had felt a moment's sadness at Valerie's loss but the death of her husband, David, had occurred far away in Canada. She had dismissed the event and moved on to more pressing matters.

Now this letter had awakened feelings she had tried to suppress; memories too painful to contemplate.

Suzanne's gentle tap at the door interrupted this disturbing train of thought.

Zoe stood up and resumed her normal posture, adopting her business persona again as if she were pulling on a magical garment that protected her from external onslaughts.

There was work to do.

Two.

"Did you get a letter from Valerie?"

"Yes, just today. I assume we both did."

"Right. What do you make of it?"

"Well, there's not much to go on. Just the location and a date."

"Are you thinking of going?"

"A free holiday in the Lake District! Are you kidding? Of course I would love it, but how, that's the question? I have work and Carla's living here since her separation and I already booked my week off for September."

"I know what you mean, Corinne, and yet it would be a great chance to see Valerie over here. She's been pretty much silent since before Dave died. I feel badly that I didn't make it to the funeral, or since then, for that matter."

"Don't beat yourself up, Sandra. We both have commitments. Are you still babysitting your grandkids?"

"A couple of days a week now. I could get a

substitute if I needed to.

We used to be such close friends when Grace was alive. I think it's a shame we have let that drop."

"Time marches on, Sandra! Things change. You should go if you want to, of course."

"Will you think about it, Corinne? It's only a few days and it's a really nice offer from Val."

"I'll think about it, but I doubt it's possible."

"Talk soon, then?"

"OK. Bye."

*

Corinne Carstairs put down the phone with a sigh. It had been a while since she and Sandra had talked. These days they had nothing much in common.

As far as she was concerned, Sandra Halder was one of the lucky ones. After her three daughters arrived in quick succession, she had enjoyed the privilege of being a stay-at-home mum.

Her hubby Ian worked long hours as a city planner to support his family and Sandra had the leisure to spend her days around regular TV programs and neighbourhood coffee mornings. To make it all easier, her girls had married young and produced grandchildren. Even after the house was empty, she had never taken up the teaching career she had trained for when she and Valerie met in Teachers College in Glasgow long ago.

Jealous? Sure she was.

Medical nurse and intake receptionist at the biggest hospital for miles around was a job that ranged from deadly boring to absolute chaos when things went wrong. A raging city fire or a multiple accident meant everyone on staff did double duty until the emergency was over. There were days when Corinne Carstairs wanted to throw her identification name tag in the rubbish bin and run screaming from the building; when smiling reassuringly at one more lost patient and giving instructions that a moron could read for himself, was too much to bear.

Lately the pressure had become almost epic. Arthur insisted she was menopausal and it was obvious he was avoiding her at night with the excuse that she tossed and turned so much he could not get a wink of sleep. He spent most nights in the spare bedroom, still decorated with Colin's trophies and soccer memorabilia.

Having Carla moping around at home didn't help things. She seemed traumatized about her marriage breakdown and incapable of washing a dish or making a cup of tea for her mother. Arthur was sympathetic to her for some reason. Of course, he had no clue what had caused the split. Corinne, on the other hand, had heard all about it in endless phone calls reaching well into the nights when Carla first decided marriage was not what she had bargained for.

Really? Who knew what they were in for after the procession down the aisle? There were no guarantees.

There was no peace at home, or at work.

A week away in the comparative freedom of the Lake District sounded like paradise. Valerie had always been a motherly kind of older woman, taking her cue from Grace who was almost saintly in her compassion. The one thing Corinne longed for right at the moment was a soft motherly bosom to enfold her, a warm hand to pat her back and a soothing voice to tell her all would be well.

Darn! Just thinking about it had made her cry. That was a sure sign she was going loopy.

She glanced at her watch and saw she would have to move fast to get to the hospital in time for her shift.

If things were quiet for a change, she could

possibly work on a fantasy plan to escape to Ambleside.

*

Sandra Halder found herself thinking about Grace Morton. It was not for the first time, of course.

In a strange way, it was like Grace was as much a presence now she was gone, as she had been in life.

It was Valerie who was Sandra's oldest friend and Valerie who had brought Grace into their lives.

Grace was the type of person anyone would be lucky to meet once in a lifetime. She was totally special. Unforgettable. Yet she was the kind of woman you might walk past without ever knowing what you would have missed. Her appearance was not remarkable at all. She was of average height and a bit above average weight. Sandra took some comfort from that fact, as she was still in the process of 'losing that baby weight' years after the last 'baby' had left the nest.

Grace's real quality was internal, not external. She had a beautiful soul. It was that simple. She radiated genuine goodness. Sandra had never heard Grace say a bad word about anyone and she was always ready to help out whenever she was needed.

She had appeared at Sandra's door that morning when Joanne was a new arrival and both Sharon and Rachel had streaming colds. It was one of those moments when you had no clue how to cope and strength was running out. Grace took in the situation with a glance, put the little girls into a steaming bath with bubbles and toys and waved Sandra off to nap with the baby.

When she emerged from the bedroom, refreshed and rested, the girls were clean, fed, and no longer crying. They were cuddling on the sofa, with thumbs in mouths, while Grace read them a story. It was a kind of miracle and Sandra never forgot that timely rescue, or the rescuer.

Valerie and Sandra had attended Grace's funeral. They were both appalled at the suddenness of Grace's death but the sight of a young Zoe almost prostrate had shocked them even more. They had felt so sorry for Zoe and tried to bring her into their circle. It had worked for a while but Zoe was so much younger than them and soon it was clear how different from her mother she seemed to be.

Zoe moved on and then there were three: Val, Sandra and Corinne.

When Val and Dave moved to Canada, the circle was finally broken.

And now, Valerie was sending out a call to mend that break. Sandra searched her heart and knew there had been something important missing in her life. The company of old and dear friends was a special part of life that was lost in the hassles of family concerns. Yes, it was there somewhere in the background but immediate priorities of daily living took over and time went by so quickly.

Once, she and Val had been so close. The very day they discovered they were room-mates in the Teachers College residence, they had bonded together as strangers in the big city. Their motto was 'together against all comers'.

Sandra felt out of her depth in the college classes and terrified in school situations. Without Valerie's support she would never have made it through the three years of their training. When they graduated together, she believed they were sisters forever. Now she knew how rare that feeling was.

Could it be time to make a space in her daily routines to renew old friendships?

The television was flickering in the background. Sandra's favourite show was on; reruns of Oprah's old daily series.

Suddenly she knew what to do. Oprah always said, live your best life and take hold of chances to improve. She would write to Valerie today, before she could change her mind.

Three.

Valerie Westwood checked the phone again and looked in her mailbox although the day's delivery had arrived three hours before. Even taking the distance from the United Kingdom into account, surely she could have expected some replies by now?

What if no one accepted her invitation? She felt as if that would seriously diminish her husband's generosity and leave a gap in her plans that she had no idea how she would fill.

Two days before he died, David had asked for the morphine drip to be disconnected and despite considerable pain, he claimed back his clarity of mind for a brief time so he could tell his wife what he wanted. Valerie would never forget those precious final moments as they sat face to face and hand in hand for the last time.

"Val, I have taken you to hell and back and I never said thank you as I should have."

She shook her head and would have protested

but he cleared his throat and gripped her hand to stop her words.

"You gave me all your love and devotion and shielded the boys from the worst of what was happening. It will soon be over for us. I am glad to go, my dear girl. It is enough."

Tears fell on his hand from her bowed face. She did not have the heart to deny anything he was saying.

He signalled for a sip of water and continued. His voice was weaker now.

"You must find happiness in any way you can, my darling. Move on. The boys and their families are looked after in my will. I want you to use all the money that's left for yourself. Go where you want. Think of yourself for a change. I loved you when we first met. I love you more now, and always."

The effort left him depleted and the pain returned with a vengeance. Valerie recognized the signs and left quickly to summon the nurse to his bedside.

David Westwood never regained consciousness.

*

The weeks that followed were a blur. Brian took

over the funeral arrangements that his father had carefully organized. People came and went from the house. Food and cards were left.

Days and nights passed. She was deep in a dark place, silent and alone but it was, in the end, a place of healing. So much of her life had been devoted to David's recovery that she had lost the ability to recognize her own needs.

It was not until she awoke one winter morning with deep snow on the ground and that peculiar stillness that indicates everything in the city has come to a halt, that she finally acknowledged the fact that she, Valerie Westwood, was still alive in the midst of the silence.

She had immediately craved sound and life around her. She turned on the radio and switched on the gas fire. She went around the bedroom and picked up discarded clothes from the floor, dropping them in a hamper as she went.

Then she tackled the living room and laughed out loud. Not much living had been happening in that room for weeks. There were cups floating with dregs of tea and coffee, a few plates with the remains of casseroles left by well-meaning neighbours, and a scattering of empty cookie and chip bags. She could not remember how these had got there or what the contents had tasted like.

The kitchen was remarkably clean but the refrigerator was stuffed with uneaten food, most of which would have to be thrown out.

On the hall table, the phone pulsed with a red light signalling messages unanswered. A pile of cards and notes had overbalanced and tumbled onto the floor. Had she taken this mail inside the house then ignored it? For how long?

On her way back into the living room she caught sight of a stranger in the mirror and staggered back in shock. Who was this woman with straggling grey hair, sunken eyes and a haunted face? The woman raised her hand to cover her mouth and Valerie saw her own wedding rings on that hand.

This was the final jolt that catapulted her into the bathroom and a hot shower. No one had ever seen her in this unkempt condition. She shivered to think what her sons or daughters-in-law would have thought had they found her like this. She was grateful that none of them lived close enough to pop over for a quick visit.

As the soothing water ran down her body, she wept the salt tears that washed away the pain and sorrow and brought her back to the realization that she was still alive and she had a mission.

David's final words to her demanded a response.

Move on. Find happiness. Think of yourself. Go where you want.

*

Winter had melted into an early spring before she was ready to act. There had been a backlog of phone calls and letters and visits to the boys and their families to reassure them she was, indeed, coping.

There were offers of dinners and days away and cottages to share but most of these she had politely turned down. Figuring out what she wanted to do with the rest of her life demanded a great deal of quiet thinking time.

First, there was the house. After the boys married, the house outside London, in Kilworth, that had sheltered four for so many happy years seemed empty and echoing. Superimposed on good memories were others tainted by Dave's cancer treatments and their aftermath. For too long there had been no energy left over for household repairs or the replacements and the renovations that the old house required.

Halfway through carpet removal, painting work and the disposal of outmoded furniture, drapes, clothing and decorative items, Valerie came to the conclusion that she was, in effect, preparing her home for sale.

This surprising discovery revitalized her energies and she set to the task of emptying shelves of ancient books and clearing out the stored basement boxes. She took photos of china sets and souvenirs of boyhood treasures and sent them to her children. It was no surprise when the response was to give these to a charity as they were not required. She did as requested and soon found the clearer, more spacious look of the house was both calming and invigorating.

Second, came the personal overhaul. All the hard work in the house had worn away the pounds accumulated during the years of nursing duties. The hair that she had pinned out of her way while she scrubbed floors and washed cupboard shelves, now demanded some attention.

A trip to a well-advertised local spa resolved the question of what improvements in her appearance might be possible. The beautiful, young girls who inhabited the various departments of the spa, did not seem fazed by the middle-aged body and neglected skin and hair she presented to them. They gently cleansed, buffed, moisturized and applied a series of potions and pastes while praising any positive feature they could find in their protégé.

Valerie learned she had lovely pale hands and nails and her hair was fine-textured and naturally wavy. According to these experts, she had somehow acquired a well-proportioned figure.

The new woman who emerged from a series of spa sessions, was almost unrecognizable to herself.

Valerie's confidence rose as she saw in her own mirror, (not as forgiving as the ones she had used in the spa but flattering nevertheless), a slender attractive person with short, fair hair, polished nails and skin that glowed with the application of careful make-up. Her brows were plucked into submission, her eyelashes darkened and her lips had been enlarged by a lipstick that somehow supplied colour with added volume. Massage had even improved the skin of her neck and chest remarkably.

It would have been ungrateful and uncharitable to refuse to make use of this newly-refurbished

Valerie.

It was part of what Dave had wished for her. Move on. Find happiness.

Happiness was a far-off goal for now, but satisfaction could be found in the new clothes she needed to complement her updated image. At first this seemed like a simple task. Buying clothes was something in which she had definitely had prior experience. But time had passed since then and she found herself bemused by the different styles and colours she saw everywhere.

What would suit her now? Where should she shop? Some stores she had formerly patronized had actually disappeared from the retail scene. Eaton's was long gone and Sears' stores were vanishing.

Even Zellers, where she had once found good bargains, had been replaces by a giant Target which now seemed to cater exclusively to very young shoppers.

She was wandering around the downtown streets looking for inspiration when rain began to fall and she stepped back into a doorway to shelter until the shower had passed. The rain pursued her there and threatened to soak a new pair of shoes, the one item she had felt confident enough to buy. Entering the store was a convenient way to keep dry and pass the time.

It was a narrow shop receding into the back area but the colourful mannequins made up for the lack of space. She walked forward to the first display and saw at once that the entire outfit was exactly what she had been hoping to find. There was a soft jacket in a plum colour matched to a draped skirt with a reasonable length instead of the miniskirts she had been seeing everywhere. The scarf around the mannequin's neck was delightful and the purse with a long strap complemented the entire outfit. It was perfect!

The reason was soon evident. A mature woman emerged from the back of the store and enquired if she could be of some help. One glance demonstrated that the owner's own clothing was the model for her displays.

Valerie left the store, some hours later, with several bags of new clothes and an invitation to call any time for a consultation or delivery. She knew she had made a new friend and ally.

With the outer transformation completed, Valerie Westwood had to tackle the next step.

Where did she want to go?

This decision was much more difficult. Having

recently visited her sons and their families, she knew she was not needed in their lives. Her two lovely daughters-in-law were good wives and mothers. Each of them had a mother of her own nearby to call upon in emergencies. To her sons' children, Valerie was 'your Gran from Ontario. Your Dad's mother, remember?' The truth was that she had been isolated by David's medical needs for so long that she had missed the vital early years of her grandchildren's childhoods. It was too late to catch up now. Perhaps when they were older she could try again.

So, where did she want to be in the meantime?

The family home was not yet up for sale but finding somewhere new in the town should not be a problem. There were condo complexes of every size and shape popping up all over the place.

Is that what she wanted? A simpler life?

*

One beautiful May evening as she sat on the front porch with a glass of wine in hand and a cashmere shawl around her shoulders, she thought about where she had felt the most happy. She had already excluded the years with the babies around her knees in this home and later when she took up teaching again. The important thing now was to look forward.

And yet, a memory emerged that had a powerful link to both the past and to David. When the boys were in college and busy with work and their friends in the summer months, she and David had gone back to Britain for holidays. It was always so reassuring to travel to places they had once known so well. Places where there were no language problems or strange money to deal with; where there were family members to visit if they chose to, or new areas to explore on their own.

They had started in Scotland and revisited the scenes of their respective childhoods and the early days of their marriage. Inevitably, there were disappointments. They say you can never go home again. The church where they were wed had been demolished. The old school, once such an imposing building seemed small, old and shabby now. Rows of shops that, in memory required a long walk, were reduced to nothing from a car trip. All was changed.

So they followed the tourist routes around the coastal towns. They found castles and glens, vast moors and spectacular mountains. They got lost a few times but laughed at their mistakes and often discovered quiet places off the beaten track they would never had seen otherwise.

David was a seeker of unusual crafts and jewellery. She used to joke that he could smell out craft shops from miles away and he was seldom wrong.

Before the airlines lowered the boom on luggage allowances, many treasures, large and small, were flown back to Canada to decorate their home.

It was on one of their trips to the Borders that they had decided to take a detour to the Lake District in the north-west of England, not far from the Scottish town of Carlisle. They had heard tales of the wonders of this part of England. In fact, so many recommendations and fervid comments along the lines of 'Oh, you *must* go there!', that they had felt reluctant to add to the songs of praise.

How could any place be so wonderful? It was sure to be another disappointment.

Of course, they could not have been more wrong. From the first moment when they saw the mountains rising into the sky above them, they were hooked. Not that the mountains in Scotland were any less magnificent. Those northern rugged peaks were forbidding and largely inaccessible to the casual walker. In the Lake District, fells and mountains were threaded by well-maintained paths. Signs denoting Public Footpaths would lead through woods to hillsides and then ever upward to grand and glorious peaks. Achieving the climb was satisfying and so was the knowledge that by following the path downward, flat ground would safely be found again.

Valerie was enchanted. Every time she stopped to catch her breath, by simply turning her head she would see amazing views over lakes and into the far distance. It was truly a magical place.

Best of all, she thought, those adventures had been shared by David; a younger version of her husband who had then been fit and energetic. The fresh air gave them both an appetite for food, for love, for life itself. They returned home to Canada renewed and invigorated.

That was then.

Valerie wondered why the memories had come to her with such vivid impact. Then she realized these were happy times in a happy place. So, was this where she should be?

Immediately, she retreated from the idea.

Holidays were not real life. Summer days were not the same as winter months. A year in the mountains where the towns were spread apart and facilities could be scarce in bad weather would be stepping back to an environment that had originally driven her and David to leave for Canada. Their lives were in Canada. Their children and grandchildren were here.

She could not abandon all that. Those links may be fragile at the moment but they were vital links.

She knew no one in that beautiful part of England. Being alone there would be worse than wandering around in this empty mausoleum of a house.

But why be alone there?

Life consisted of many links. Family was one, but there were important links to old friends.

Why not invite Sandra and Corinne, and even Zoe, to join her in the Lake District? They were all living in Scotland or England. Not far for them to travel and a chance for Valerie to revisit a happier time in her life.

The idea caught fire in her mind. It could be wonderful to spend a week together renewing old memories and getting caught up with all that she had missed. She would use the money

Dave had left her to find a place large enough for all of them.

Once decided, the plan went swiftly forward. Letters were written and sent to the addresses she had used last Christmas. She would follow up with phone calls if necessary, but she wanted each of the women to have time to consider her invitation without the pressure of having to provide an instant reply.

Using the internet to survey the many holiday rental options she soon found a suitable apartment with ample space for four. It was situated on a steep hillside in Ambleside, a town she was familiar with from the old days. More research produced a car rental firm whose associates assured her they had a 'people carrier' sufficient in size to accommodate 'her party'. She had a moment of dismay thinking of the many times David had taken on this task for her and driven her everywhere she requested. Now it was all up to her. The next thought passing through her mind was that both the car and the self-catering apartment might prove to be more spaces much too large for one, should none of her old friends accept her offer.

Defying the odds that presented themselves, she packed a case and booked a hotel for three days before the designated week so she could get oriented to the area again and look for restaurants, food stores and interesting locations for the group to visit.

Everything was in place.

Who would be joining her?

Four.

Another week went by before the first letter arrived.

Predictably, it was from Sandra. Her oldest and dearest friend began by apologizing profusely for her neglect of the last few years and Valerie had to read fast through this part until she reached the important information. Yes, Sandra would be joining her for the week. She ended by writing she did not think Corinne would be available but hoped Valerie would not be too upset if it was only the two of them.

The very thought of time alone with Sandra made Valerie's heart sing. They knew each other so well. Years between their meetings meant nothing compared to the years they had spent together while their lives and careers were forming. Marriage and children were shared experiences. Valerie's two boys and Sandra's three girls were a constant source of comment between them. They had even speculated about the possibility that one of the boys might marry one of the girls and so cement the families together forever.

That was not to be. When Valerie and David made the decision to emigrate, the distance severed the children's prior closeness and the lives of all five went in different directions.

This thought made Valerie return to the boxes in her house labelled, 'To be kept'. She found the one containing family photographs and extracted the most recent ones of her boys and the grandkids which she had printed from her camera after her recent visits.

She made a note to ask Sandra to do the same for her girls and their families. Photographs were not the same as the frequent occasions to share her grandkids' lives that Sandra had always been blessed with, but they were an excellent way to start conversations about how things changed over time and Valerie wondered if those conversations would provide a way for her to accept this disappointment in her own life. Did her friends also have areas of dissatisfaction? Places where things had not turned out as expected? Surely everyone had sorrows of this type. She thought about the comfort of sharing sorrows and the possible solutions that might present themselves when two, or three, female minds worked together. It might be an idea to make preparations for this in the same way as she had planned to survey the places to visit in the Lake District.

She set out to make a list of questions to promote discussion then wondered if that could be perceived as intrusive. And yet, it would be an opportunity to move conversation onto a different level; a deeper stratum where truths and secrets could be mined.

After all, if it turned out that Corinne could join them, it would make a fund of information about three long-term marriages and the peaks and pitfalls of such unusual unions. These days 'starter' marriages of only a few years seemed to be acceptable.

She struggled with this dilemma for three more days and then decided to make a list but to reserve it until, and unless, the perfect opportunity arose.

The List.
- If you could talk to your teenage self, what advice would you offer her?
- Did you marry the right man?
- What kept you going during the rough patches?

- What is your biggest fear?

She put the list in her luggage together with the photographs and a few pairs of shoes. At this point she discovered two things. First, the case was already feeling heavy. Second, she would need light climbing boots and an expandable walking stick, or two. Although she was aware the heights she had once scaled with David would now be beyond her capacity, she was determined to try for some of the more modest climbs, if only to give her friend, or friends, a chance to feel that liberating sense of exhilaration and achievement when released from the confines of earthbound civilization for a brief time.

To solve the first problem Valerie went off on a shopping expedition to find a lighter, more manoeuvrable suitcase. This involved much hefting of samples and checking of sizes.

After some time she decided on a very light, full-sized case with wheels that turned in all directions.

This feature had been demonstrated to her by a helpful assistant. It allowed the traveller to escort the case through any area with a flat surface with only a minimum amount of force.

The case almost walked by itself and eliminated the need to haul it behind her back with no clue who might be tripping over it.

The footwear issue, however, was not so easy to resolve. In the end, she shelved the difficulty and determined to find the required items during her advance survey. If her memory served, every town in the Lake District had a plethora of hiking , camping, outdoor clothing and equipment stores.

*

As every necessary item was packed in the new case and the package of print reservations grew in size, Valerie could feel excitement growing inside her. It was a pleasant sense of anticipation and yet, the plan was not complete.

Nothing had arrived from Corinne or Zoe. She knew the latter invitation had been a long shot right from the beginning but some instinct told her to keep hoping, for Zoe's sake. Valerie had long suspected there was something wrong in her god-daughter's life.

Corinne was another matter. Her connection to Corinne was not based on long association like it was with Sandra. In fact, it was David's cancer that had brought Corinne into their lives.

Shortly after they received the diagnosis of a rare and unusual cancer, David and Valerie discovered there was only one hospital in the world that would accept him for an experimental research program. The protocol required David to be a patient for three days every week over a period of six weeks. As this hospital was in Birmingham, England, they made the difficult decision to leave Canada and stay together in England during the procedure.

Brian was old enough to supervise his younger brother and they trusted both their son and his sensible girlfriend, to act with responsibility and maturity.

Corinne was introduced to them as their medical contact person on their first hospital visit. They were still jet lagged from the flight and worried about where they would live and how David would respond to the risky treatment. Corinne immediately took over. She offered them a room in her home, a ride to the hospital and, best of all, she made an instant connection to David's dark sense of humour assuring him they would become friends in the most personal way during his ordeal but she was not on duty at home should he need his head held over the toilet.

The laugh that broke the tension at this statement set the tone for the next six weeks. Corinne kept David's spirits up, called him Dave or Davie, made sure he got to know her husband Arthur and reassured Valerie whenever her hope of a cure faltered.

It was a very worrying time for Valerie. There was little she could do besides support the workers. She did housework happily as it kept her busy on days David was in the hospital. She cooked healthy meals for all of them and had many long talks with Arthur over the dinner table when Corinne was on night duty. Valerie had asked Arthur why Corinne was so generous with her home. Did she do this for all out-of-town patients? He replied that it was an occasional thing and helped to keep them afloat financially. Arthur was in construction work as a project supervisor and their two children were not living at home at the moment. Carla was at university and Colin was in the army overseas, hence the spare rooms.

Valerie was always on hand when David and Corinne arrived back from their gruelling days in the hospital. David would be pale and weak but he managed a laugh when Corinne helped him out of the car and threatened to get him a

Zimmer frame if he could not manage the front steps by himself.

Valerie watched the effect of Corinne's tough-love challenges. David squared his shoulders, took a deep breath and slowly climbed the steps to the top with a grin of accomplishment on his face.

From these observations Valerie learned not to fuss and fawn over the patient. She kept her worries for midnight hours and her estimation of Corinne grew by leaps and bounds.

David survived the treatment and returned to Canada with a new lease on life and a new friend for life in Corinne. As far as Valerie was concerned, Corinne was lifesaver to both of them and she remained close to the couple for the next decade until David's condition deteriorated.

*

"So, you've made the decision to go, Sandra?"

"Yes, Corinne. I feel I can't let Val down but I wish you would come with me. Couldn't you switch your week off just this once?"

"Believe me, I've been thinking about it. It's absolute pandemonium in the hospital this month. It's like every kid with a peanut allergy has descended on us and every adult with a serious illness suddenly moved into a critical phase at the same time. There are beds in the hallways and doctors dropping like flies from the stress."

"Corinne, that sounds awful! You must be exhausted! You definitely need this break. Will you promise to try to come and join us if things calm down at the hospital in the next few weeks?"

"Can't promise anything but if a miracle happens, count me in."

"That's good enough for now. Please take care of yourself. Give my best to Arthur and Carla."

"I'll do that."

Much good it will do, she thought, as she put down her mobile phone. Arthur was in a worse state than she was. The summer months were their only chance to get ahead financially. Winters in the building trade were uncertain at best and he was trying to accumulate enough cash to float them through the bad weather periods. This meant long days on construction sites solving delivery problems and searching for proficient workers who could be persuaded to stay. He was always under the gun time-wise and she could see the pressure building up.

Corinne had no more time to think about Valerie's offer. She reheated a two-day-old casserole, left a note about it on the kitchen table then went to bed. If Carla wanted to eat she had better do something to turn the mush into a meal. Corinne had eaten something hours before in the hospital cafeteria but was now too tired to put food before her desperate need for sleep.

The next two days at the hospital were even worse. A doctor actually screamed for help in frustration at not being able to move a patient's bed into the elevator by himself. Two nurses ran to his aid and Corinne, sensing a melt-down on the way, gave the job of monitoring her patient's drip to the nurses' aide beside her and fled out into the corridor closing the door behind her. It would do no good for patients to hear the staff freaking out.

The doctor in question was one of the new batch who had been working unconscionable hours all week.

He saw Corinne approaching and yelled at her to get down to A&E immediately. The elevator doors closed before she could ask exactly where in Emergency she was needed. She took the stairs for speed. As soon as the heavy fire door clanged shut behind her she stopped and dropped down on the top step. The sound as the door echoed in the empty stairwell had hit her like a bad omen of some kind. It seemed to signify an ending. Didn't they say a door closing in life meant somewhere a window was opening? She was too exhausted to examine that saying.

Folding her arms across her knees, she bent her head for a moment and prayed for strength. She inhaled the disinfectant on her arms and rested her weary eyes on the bright pattern of her uniform trousers. The cold from the stone step soon seeped up into her skin and she would have cried if she had any tears left.

"I can't keep doing this," she told herself. "I am getting too old for this madness."

The moment's pause gave her back some small fund of energy and she sped down the flights to Emergency on the ground level. The situation there was no better. Porters and aides were scurrying around while doctors barked out orders and handled the machines that would save lives or at least delay life-threatening damage.

Corinne pumped some sterilising foam onto her

hands and headed to the first of the screened areas.

It looked like a woman in early labour. There was blood on the bed but the nurse signalled to Corinne that everything was in hand.

The next booth held a boy with a bad case of hives. The doctor by his side, glanced over at Corinne and gave her a strange look. She knew Dr. Drew well but could not interpret his meaning.

She moved to the next station where there was a lot of noise. This patient must have been admitted recently as the flurry of activity around his bed had not yet settled into the calm state indicating everything had been done to keep him, or her, stable. She saw legs thrashing around so she went forward to hold the legs and steady the patient for the oxygen mask that was about to be placed over his face. For a split second, the nurse and doctor turned toward Corinne and froze in place. She got a sudden instinct of danger of some kind, then they resumed their work on the patient and as they moved away from him, the feeling of danger merged into panic. The figure lying on the bed was her own husband Arthur.

It was her worst nightmare come true but

training took hold very quickly and she pushed her emotions aside until she could be sure her husband was all right.

A nod to the doctor in charge assured him she was able to cope. He handed her a syringe pack and she automatically ripped it open and prepared the injection. At the same time she was assessing the patient's injuries.

Broken collar bone and shoulder.

Blood and swelling.

Possible fractured pelvis

Semi-conscious.

Serious accident. {Was anyone else involved?)

"What happened here?"

The ER nurse was feeling Arthur's legs for further bruising or fractures but she replied at once.

"He was brought in about ten minutes ago by ambulance. We tried to contact you.

Scaffolding collapsed on the building site and your husband was in the wrong place at the wrong time. The morphine will soon cut the pain then we'll set the shoulder and put a cast on his arm.

All standard stuff. It looks worse than it is. Go off and get a cup of tea. Sugar for shock; you know the drill. He's going up to X-ray now.

Check back in half an hour."

The nurse gave her a push in the direction of the exit doors. Corinne stumbled away and felt herself shaking inside and out as the shock hit. Arthur was hurt. Her brain knew it was not a life-threatening injury but it was entirely a different feeling, emotionally, when the hurt person was someone so close. Visions of what might have happened to him flooded her mind and she had to turn it off to navigate the short distance to the cafeteria.

Word had spread quickly, and one of the cafeteria women reached her before she was two steps inside the doors.

"Lean on me, Love. I've got a nice quiet table for you over here. Just sit down for a bit and I'll have tea and a pastry over to you in a jiffy."

Somehow this kindness was the undoing of Corinne. She began to shake again and knew she was on the verge of breaking down. *Have to keep strong till I've seen Arthur*, she murmured over and over like a litany as she clung on to the metal strip along the edge of the table. She focused on the cake crumbs scattered on the table top and tried to make a pattern out of them. Some were dark like chocolate, others were creamy. What kind of pastry could they have come from?

Fran, a nurse colleague of many years, found her there with the tea cup in front of her trembling in its saucer. She took in the situation immediately. It was not the first time she had had to comfort staff members when disaster overtook them. Nurses were a tight-knit group, like buddies on the front line in a war zone and Fran thought that was an apt description for the current situation in the hospital.

"Right, Corinne! I am here to help. I'll put this blanket around your shoulders. Just get this tea down you and we'll go and find Arthur and soon the two of you can go home in a taxi."

Fran secretly thought her friend looked as if she, rather than her husband, was the patient. She had that drawn, unconnected look of shock setting in. Fran had heard all about Carla's lack of cooperation at home and hoped the young woman would see that she now had to step up to the plate with both parents needing help for some time. She also hoped Corinne would stay at home and get some rest. She was much too conscientious about her job and lately, there had been a few mistakes which were not serious but demonstrated that this nurse needed some TLC of her own.

Five.

Valerie Crestwood was waiting for the cab to take her to the airport shuttle service when her phone rang. She had already spoken to Brian and John, stopped the newspaper delivery, hired a gardening maintenance company to attend to the lawn and flowerbeds, left reminder notes with her neighbours and notified the bank that she was going to be spending money overseas.

Who could be calling at this late date?

"Valerie where are you?"

"Corinne! What's happened? How is Arthur? I am flying to England today. I thought I wouldn't hear from you again."

"Everything has changed, Val. Arthur is doing very well. His construction company boss has claimed his insurance for accident coverage and Arthur can stay at home with pay until he's fit to work again.

There's also the chance of compensation for neglect by the scaffolding firm."

"Good news, Corinne! I am so glad for you and Arthur. I know you were worried about money."

"The best part is, I am coming to join you in the Lake District! Arthur says Carla will look after him and he says I need to take a proper break. The hospital switched my week off for me and I am coming!!"

"Oh, Corinne, I can't tell you how happy I am about this. I'll see you there in a few days. Sandra will be pleased too."

"All girls together again. Just like the old days."

"Wonderful! Oh, there's my cab. Have to run. Bye for now."

"Bye, Val, and thank you."

*

The happy news kept Valerie going during the long night and morning of travel. She arrived in Manchester Airport, collected her luggage from the carousel and trudged through the airport to the train station connector line that would eventually take her to Kendal and the car hire firm.

It was more like a slow commuter train than a high speed service but as she had entered early on the route, she was able to settle into a window seat and ignore the comings and goings of students, workers and shoppers who stayed on for only a few stops. It was good to catch her breath and begin to relax. She looked out of the window and saw fields dotted with white sheep. There were farms and rivers and green, green grass. When the train stopped in a small town, she was able to look along the main street from the railway bridge and see the comings and goings of rural life that spoke to her of a more measured way of living, close to the land.

Kendal lay in a valley. She remembered that from this point all roads climbed upward until all the other Lake District towns were found amidst the mountains. She longed to look out and see those mountains wherever she looked. Ontario was mostly flat and there was something about the protective effect of heights around one that gave you a sense of security.

"I to the hills will lift mine eyes, from whence doth come mine aid." The old hymn sang in her head and soon she felt the fatigue drop away. She was here and it was all coming together perfectly just as she had hoped. David would be pleased.

A driver from the car firm loaded her luggage as soon as she stepped into the small parking lot just outside the Oxenholme station. By the time the train had roared off on its journey north again, she was heading to Kendal where she signed the car hire rental papers, received a quick run through of her rental car's features and then she was in a stream of traffic heading uphill out of the town. Driving on the left was not a problem when she merged into the busy road but she was aware she would have to be alert on some occasions when entering a road without other traffic to remind her.

All was going smoothly so far. After a few kilometres she was onto the familiar road to Ambleside skirting Windermere town. Soon Lake Windermere was on her left and she was smiling widely as each remembered sight came into view and vanished behind the car.

The day was bright and the air fresh with moisture from the expanse of blue water. She travelled on to Grasmere to the hotel that had been their favourite, set beside the lake of the same name. The parking was in front of the hotel and she had to claim two spots since she was not yet used to the dimensions of this new, large, vehicle which handled well and gave the driver an excellent view of the road ahead; a major advantage on these older winding roads.

The receptionist welcomed her like a long lost friend from Canada which Valerie thought must be the result of a database of guest names, rather than an excellent memory.

The hotel was of the comfortable and slightly old-fashioned variety much favoured by repeat customers from parts of Scotland and Yorkshire as well as further south in England. The rooms were warm and clean with all the necessary amenities but the features that made this hotel exceptional were the food, always of a high standard and beautifully presented, and the large dining room with windows on two sides displaying amazing views of mountainside and lake.

Valerie had a quick wash and unpacked just enough to see her through two days. Then she made her way into the lounge where tables and chairs were ready for more casual meals. If she had been less tired she would have eaten lunch on the wide terrace and enjoyed the fresh air but she promised herself that treat for Saturday. A pot of coffee, served with a jug of hot milk in the English style, wakened her up and a delicious ham sandwich full of English mustard and shredded salad greens amply satisfied her hunger.

She was relishing her second cup of coffee when she noticed two women seated nearby. She did not feel nosy about watching them as the women were so involved in their conversation that they were unaware of anyone around them. Their voices rose and fell interspersed with laughter. Valerie heard the word 'Vancouver' and surmised that one of them must be from British Columbia. A closer look convinced her that the two women were related. It was not too obvious at first. The younger one had dark hair cut close to her head while the older one's hair was mostly grey. The resemblance was more about the shape of their faces and the way they reached out to touch each other when they were sharing a laugh.

How lovely! Valerie thought. It was her deep regret that she had not had either a daughter or a close daughter-in-law to share the intimate moments women seemed to need in order to thrive in life.

She turned away with a smile on her face. Soon she would have two close friends to talk with for an entire week. What could be more wonderful?

Fully refreshed, Valerie collected her purse and went out to reacquaint herself with Grasmere village. She knew the historical landmarks, like the ancient church where the Wordsworth family worshipped and in whose graveyard they were buried. Those would be same as ever. She wandered around the twisting narrow roads, dodging visitors who stopped to look in the shop windows of a variety of boutique stores and reminding herself to beware of stepping out into the roadway and into the path of passing cars.

She soon found the café at the riverside which David had loved and was pleased to see it was unchanged. She could picture David throwing crumbs from his scone to the mallard ducks clustering down below. This special place was already on her list of 'must see' sites for Sandra and Corinne.

The tiny Grasmere Gingerbread shop was still selling its wares and a variety of large hotels still took up a considerable amount of the town's real estate.

Was there anything new in Grasmere since her last visit?

She stopped to check inside another tiny place sheltering in the corner by a wall. It was a

National Trust Shop. Memories returned of Dove Cottage visits and an old house at Townend, up a scary steep lane, where a coal fire always burned and everything was kept as it was in the nineteenth century.

She had let her National Trust membership lapse many years before but it was in here she found a place that could be interesting for Corinne and Sandra as well as something new for herself. A poster informed Valerie that Allan Bank had been gifted to the Trust's care in 1920 but had only recently returned to them after a long period of rental. The house and extensive grounds were a short walk from Valerie's hotel and she decided it would be a definite attraction to be included in the week's outings. Valerie added Allan Bank to the list on a small notebook she carried in her purse. Her boys had always groaned when she brought out the notebook whenever they travelled together but they were frequently glad to consult her notes when arguments arose about where and when something had happened. The notebook was an old habit. It was probably redundant nowadays but old habits die hard.

*

Dinner at The Gold Rill commenced with hot savouries and cold drinks, served in the lounge, while guests perused the menu and made their meal selection. Valerie had managed to snatch a nap before showering and changing clothes so she felt better than expected after the plane journey and all the other items to be attended to on her first day. She found a table near the fireplace and watched the other guests, mostly in groups of four, chat about their day's adventures which seemed to consist of climbing peaks and hiking on obscure trails. She would not have guessed some of them were fit enough for such pursuits, but appearances can deceive.

She recognised the couple she had noticed earlier in the day. The two women were seated nearby and still involved in animated conversation.

Soon, a smartly dressed young girl approached Valerie and asked if she had chosen her dinner dishes. Valerie read out her selection for the four courses and had to raise her voice since the large group to her left were obviously enjoying a family reunion. She had just lifted her glass to sip the gin and tonic she had ordered when she was approached from the table to her right, by the younger of the two women who she had identified as the Canadian mother and daughter.

"Please excuse this interruption. Are you dining alone? My mother and I overheard your dinner order and we were wondering if you happen to be Canadian? You see my mother is here from Canada and I am Canadian originally. We would love it if you would join us. Eating on your own is such a boring thing, isn't it? I am Jeanette McLennan from Oban and my mother is Jean from Vancouver."

Valerie almost choked on her drink. Surprise was written all over her face but she was equally pleased at this offer to be saved from a lengthy, lonely meal.

"Why, I would be so pleased to join you. How very kind of you both!"

"Right then! I'll go and sort out the tables in the dining room while you chat to my mother."

With that, she was gone. Valerie looked over at the other occupant, now smiling in a welcoming manner and waving her hand to indicate her agreement.

"Don't mind Jeanette," she began, as soon as Valerie had seated herself. "She's always been impulsive. Don't feel obliged to do as she says if you would rather be alone. The truth is she's an eternally curious creature and just wants to interrogate you about Canada in case I might be exaggerating about something."

Valerie had to smile at this assessment. Jeanette certainly seemed to be unusually forward, but then she was Canadian and not as reserved as the typical English person. An evening with this interesting mother and daughter was something she would welcome.

In the next ten minutes, Valerie discovered that the mother and daughter were escaping from Oban for a few nights of luxury off on their own.

"Mom loves her grandchildren, of course, but she has not long lost my father and she needs a bit of peace and quiet. Liam is at school all day but the little one, Annette, is a chatty miss like her mother, I suppose, and with George coming and going at all hours, and my clients popping in, it's a busy household, for sure."

While Jeanette took a breath, Valerie looked into the hazel eyes of the older woman and said quietly,

"I am recently widowed also. It's a very difficult time and good that you have family with you."

There was an instant rapport between the two women and much unsaid, but deeply understood, passed from one to the other. Valerie knew they would soon find a space to compare notes in private about their respective bereavements.

Jeanette caught the glance and expressed her sympathy then changed the topic of conversation to allow Valerie to tell her story. "What brings you from Canada to the Lake District, Valerie?"

"Well, I guess I am revisiting places I once loved when my husband was alive. I have invited two old friends to join me here for a week in Ambleside. It's time for me to renew friendships and start living again."

"That's wonderful!" exclaimed Jeanette, "and exactly what *I* am telling my mother to do now that she has choices. Where are you staying in Ambleside?"

"I am renting a large apartment with two bedrooms, two bathrooms and a wrap-around balcony. I haven't seen it yet but I move in tomorrow afternoon."

Jeanette seemed puzzled by this description. "Is this apartment on a steep hillside overlooking the town with spectacular mountain views, by any chance?"

"I believe so, but I am judging from the

Lakeland's website photos, of course. Why? Do you know the place?"

"You are not going to believe this, Valerie, but a very dear friend of mine owns an apartment exactly as you have described in the Lakelands complex in Ambleside."

She turned to her mother and added, "You know about Anna Drake's story, Mom. You've been to her farmhouse in Oban with me."

A host of questions filled Valerie's mind at this revelation but the announcement for the guests to take their seats for the evening meal was given and she had to wait to ask for an explanation.

Six.

It was several minutes before Valerie could again introduce the topic of the Ambleside apartment.

First, it was necessary to appreciate the beautiful Gold Rill Hotel's dining room with windows on two adjacent sides revealing mountain views lit in the heights by the rays of the setting sun. The tables were clothed in white linen and the chairs were high-backed and upholstered for comfort to match the drapes framing the windows.

The serving staff was expert and unobtrusive but knew exactly what had been ordered for each table and produced appetizing, hot plates of food without fuss. The two delicious starter courses were consumed amid exclamations of delight. It seemed to Valerie it would be impertinent to interrupt that pleasure by asking more questions and yet, her curiosity was growing by the minute.

When the main course was almost finished, Valerie tried to steer the conversation toward the answers she wanted.

"Jeanette, did I hear your mention the name Anna Drake before?"

"That's right! She was married to the artist Lawren Drake who died unexpectedly a few years back. Is the name familiar to you?"

"Yes, it is. I live in Kilworth, a small township near London, Ontario, where both Anna and Lawren lived. I saw an exhibit of his paintings in Museum London recently and there were placards beside the works telling the story of his artist's life before Anna, and showing some of the paintings he did after they met. I was struck by the contrasting styles. After Anna there was a marked difference in his work."

"Well, for goodness sake! This is quite a coincidence, Valerie. If I am right and the apartment you have rented is the one Anna owns, you are going to see prints of some of those very paintings on the walls."

"Would there be a copy of his most famous painting, the one he did for Anna Mason that brought them together?"

Jeanette chuckled as if this question was one she had heard many times before.

"To see that one you would have to get an invitation to Anna's house near Oban. It is never removed from their bedroom and few people outside the family and close friends have ever seen it, but I can assure you it's a real work of art on so many levels. Lawren did a wonderful family portrait for George and I when the children were small and that one has many of the same qualities."

Valerie sat back and tried to absorb this most unexpected information. The rented apartment suddenly became a place of relevance beyond her immediate needs and a link to her Ontario life. It was almost as if she had been meant to stay there at this important juncture in her new beginning.

She made a mental note to find out as much as she could about Anna and Lawren Drake.

"I am amazed at this, Jeanette! What a coincidence that we should meet here. But, tell me please, if your friend Anna Drake owns this apartment why are you and Jean not using it for your holiday together?"

"Oh, it's much too big for us for these few days and I prefer to be waited on hand and foot rather than have to think of meals and clean-up. It won't be a problem for you, of course. With three women together for a week you can do exactly what you want, eat in or out, and relax without any men around and, ..." Here she paused and glanced quickly at her mother before continuing. "....... this leads me to an important question of my own. How did you and your friends meet and what is this reunion all about?"

Jean looked over at her daughter with an expression of distaste on her face.

"Jeanette! Valerie's reasons are none of your business."

"Please, Jean, don't be concerned. You have both been so open about your lives and I don't mind telling you about mine."

Valerie set the fork and knife side-by-side on her plate and sat back in her chair. She had never really explained the whole story to anyone else before and this opportunity would prepare her for a similar session with her friends.

"Well, it all started when I went to College in Glasgow to become a teacher."

"I *thought* I could hear a Scottish accent! Where were you born, Valerie?"

This time Jeanette's mother gave up with a sigh and allowed her daughter's curiosity to have free rein.

It would be up to Valerie to call a halt from now on.

"I was born in an Ayrshire village and it was

easier to live in residence at the college than to travel back and forth for three years. It was in my room at Douglas House that I first met Sandra. She was from Mull and had never been in the big city before. We made an alliance for mutual support on the very first day as room mates and that has lasted all these years despite changes in our lives and circumstances."

"A true friendship!" interjected Jean, before Jeanette could interrupt with another intrusive question.

Valerie nodded, smiled and continued.

"College was also the place where we both met a woman who would influence our lives profoundly.

Grace Morton taught child psychology and early childhood philosophy. Sandra was drawn to teaching very young children and she introduced me to Professor Morton, who she said was 'the smartest, most empathetic person she had ever had the pleasure to meet.' I never found a reason to contradict Sandra's opinion.

Perhaps because we were both in residence, we had extra time to spend after classes. Grace was generous with her time and advice and we three grew close, sharing cups of tea in her office while we debated methodologies and sought help with assignments.

We two students had heard about Dr. Michael Morton who worked long hours at Glasgow University but he was a shadowy figure to us and we jealously guarded our stolen hours without much thought for the needs of Grace's husband. That is, until the day it all changed."

Valerie stopped to sip her glass of water and sample the slice of lemon cake drizzled with raspberry coulis that had been placed in front of her while she was talking. She saw Jean elbow her daughter surreptitiously and suggest she do the same. A few moments of silence, interspersed with oohs and aahs of dessert delight, occupied a minute or two until Valerie continued. She could tell Jeanette was longing for the next installment.

"You see, we had been under the illusion that Professor Morton was an older woman of our mothers' generation. She seemed so wise that she had to have had the benefit of decades of experience but on that one day we found out how wrong we were. Grace Morton revealed a secret to us after first swearing us to secrecy. She had discovered she was pregnant after years of failing to conceive. From that moment we saw her quite differently. She was not that much older than we were and she was overjoyed to finally become a mother.

Sandra and I were thrilled to be part of the secret. We took on the role of unofficial teaching assistants and helped Professor Morton with her heavy workload wherever possible.

Grace was determined to teach as long as she could so as to retain her position. It was a three year limited assignment, as were all the college teaching positions in those days. Professors would return to the classroom after their time was up so as to be current with school conditions and methods. Grace was only one year away from the end of her term and not likely to ever get the opportunity again. It was important to her to complete her assignment.

Her flowing black gown concealed the pregnancy but Sandra and I knew how taxing her teaching became with her almost constant nausea preventing her from eating properly.

At the end of the day, we would bring soups and omelettes from the college cafeteria and try to tempt her with milkshakes and any appetising delicacies that appeared on the menu. Later on, she swore she would never have been able to persuade her husband she was coping so well had it not been for our constant support."

Jeanette could not wait to hear what happened. "Tell about the baby," she urged.

"Zoe was born in the spring of our first year at the college and Grace Morton retired to look after her daughter but our association with the family continued for several years after that. Grace was always willing to help us through our training and we babysat for the Mortons whenever they had events to attend. Zoe was my goddaughter, a role which I shared with Sandra for some years."

"So, what took you to Canada and did your friendship continue even then?"

Jean stopped Valerie from replying to Jeanette's questions by pointing out that the dining room was almost empty and guests were assembling for coffee in the adjacent sitting room.

"Oh, I do apologise for being so curious. My mother is always warning me about that but I am so interested in your story. Would you mind continuing over coffee or tea? Maybe you are too tired?"

"No, I don't mind at all but I think Jean may be ready for bed."

Jean, who had been trying to conceal her yawning, was happy to be excused. She bent to kiss her daughter, murmuring something in her ear which Valerie did not hear.

*

Coffee cups in hand, they settled into the soft cushions of a sofa in a quiet nook. A plate of foil-wrapped chocolates glinted on a low table in front of them and they sampled several between sips of an excellent coffee.

"Now, where were we?"

"You were about to say how you got from Scotland to Canada."

Valerie cleared her mouth of orange-flavoured chocolate and resumed her story.

"It was inevitable, I suppose. Once a woman finds a man she wants to marry, she adopts his family and his needs and gives them as much importance as her own. My husband David was the youngest of a family of three children, two of which had already made the move to Canada. We took a holiday to Ontario so I could meet his brother and sister and we just fell in love with the country, the weather, and the space everywhere around us. It seemed a good place to live."

"I know exactly what you mean, Valerie. I met

and married George and left my life in British Columbia behind me. I find I am separated from the friends I grew up with. The distance between us is just too far.
Did it happen to you and Sandra?"

"At first we wrote furiously and talked on the phone to bridge that distance. Sandra gave me updates on Grace and Zoe and I sent photos of our boys as they arrived.
We tried. Then Sandra's girls were born in quick succession. She gave up teaching and I had to continue with my career until David and I had a house, cars, and all the trappings of family life in Canada. Gradually the contact diminished until it was cards and notes on special occasions."

"Sad, isn't it? Yet it's the way of the world these days. I am so glad my Mom is able to visit her grandkids now. For years she wouldn't leave my father and there was no one else to look after him."
Valerie took a deep breath and realised how difficult it was going to be to move out of the corner of the sofa. If she didn't stir herself now, she was going to have to spend the night in this cozy nest.

"I'm afraid jet lag is catching up on me, Jeanette. I really have to head for bed."

"Oh, forgive me, Valerie. I know I am a terrible chatterbox. George often tells me I could talk till the cows come home. I'll go up and see if Mom has fallen asleep yet. Thank you for sharing your story with us. It's been lovely meeting you. Perhaps we'll meet again someday."

"Who knows? It's been most interesting so far. Good night."

The two women exchanged a quick hug and smiled warmly at each other. They had only met a few hours before and yet, confidences draw peopled together faster than anything else and they parted as new friends.

Seven.

<u>Saturday.</u>

The day dawned bright. Valerie was awakened by the sun streaming onto her bed. She had forgotten to close the drapes in her rush to get horizontal as soon as possible. A glance at the bedside clock revealed the fact that she had almost missed breakfast. She sank back on her pillows and decided to skip breakfast. After all, she had enjoyed a substantial meal late in the evening.

Her next thought was how busy this day would be and then she jumped up and found a casual outfit, splashed some water on her face and ran a comb through her hair. Better to start the day with some sustenance in case she was too rushed to eat later.

The dining room was almost vacant. Two tables were still occupied by guests who were finishing off their coffee and tea in preparation for leaving. Valerie turned to retreat but was stopped by the restaurant manager.

"Oh, I know it's too late," she explained. Don't worry! I'll have a snack later."

"Not at all, Madam! Please come in, you can have cereal and juice while I get your order ready. Full English? Tea or coffee? Mixed toast? Oh! There's a message waiting at your table."
Valerie selected cereal and added fruit from a large bowl of mixed, sliced fruits. She picked up a small jar of marmalade to save time later and made her way to the same table at which she had dined the night before. On her side plate she found an envelope.

Valerie we enjoyed your company last evening.
Mom says I should apologise for monopolizing the conversation but I am sure you did not mind.
We are leaving early today for shopping in Windermere and a trip to Hill Top to get Beatrix Potter books for my Annette.
Have a wonderful time with your friends. I will tell Anna about you when we get home to Oban.
You will find my contact information on the back of this note. Keep in touch.
Jeanette McLennan.

By the time she had carefully read the note, a plate of scrambled eggs with sausage, ham and half a tomato appeared before her. The smell was so appealing, she pushed the cereal aside and set to with an appetite she did not know she had. Two cups of coffee later and the last slice of toast and marmalade consumed, she felt like her holiday was about to begin in earnest. She had just enough space left for the bowl of cereal in the end, and remembered to tuck Jeanette's note into her sleeve. The information about the owner of the apartment she was about to rent would be another interesting fact to add to the week's plans.

Before she could check out the Ambleside apartment she had to shower, pack, pay the hotel bill and add to her list of places Sandra and Corinne might want to visit. She felt she had Grasmere covered but she needed a wider variety of local attractions to tempt every possible interest.

"After all, "she cautioned herself while applying some colour to her face in front of the bathroom mirror, "I can't be sure what they would like. It's been forever since I spent time with either one of them. The main thing is that they enjoy this week. I need to make each day significant."

With a final narrowing of her eyes to convey determination, she left the mirror image and resumed packing her two cases for the move to Ambleside.

While waiting in the foyer for a couple to settle their bill, Valerie spied a display of tourist brochures and pamphlets. She immediately scanned the selection and soon had a fistful of activities and events to survey later. At first glance she noted Kendal was the most likely shopping expedition as it had a High Street mall, a Marks & Spencer store, and a large outlet area on the edge of the town, called K Village.

"Every woman likes to shop," she mused, "and I have never done that in my years here with David. He was more focused on walking and climbing."

An unusual pamphlet was added to the collection when she spotted an outsized brochure for 'Blackwell: The Arts and Crafts House'. There was no time to read the whole thing but she noted that this house was near Bowness which she knew could be reached by launch or steamship from the Ambleside end of Lake Windermere. A day's outing was beginning to form in her mind until she reminded herself not to plan ahead too much. It was essential that her guests could choose according to their own preferences.

"It never hurts to be prepared!" she stated, as she tucked the handful of materials into her purse.

*

The day flew by. Valerie reacquainted herself with Ambleside's many features including the famous Apple Pie Bakery where she bought a slice of their spicy apple and devoured it in record time inhaling the delicious scents of fresh baking that permeated the small shop.

The town was busy with visitors, as happened every time a sunny day appeared. She dodged around couples with children and dogs, and kept an eye on her watch so as to retrieve her car from the parking lot before the ticket expired. She did not want to miss a moment of her first look at the apartment which would be her home for the week.

Four o'clock found Valerie poised to enter the large suite through its balcony door. She had the keys in hand with a device that gave entrance to the pool complex situated below the three apartments on the top level. She could hardly contain her excitement. Stepping onto the balcony made her stop and catch her breath. At this height, half-way up a hillside already, the view was astonishing. Directly in front of her the green slope of a mountaintop reached up to the sky. On her far right, a horseshoe of mountains gleamed in the sunlight and she could tell the valley between must lead to Grasmere through Rydal, the route she had driven in reverse after leaving the hotel earlier.

It was as if Ambleside had disappeared. Rooftops and the spire of a large church were all she could see of the town, yet, right beneath her, must be the main street with traffic and shops and pedestrians, the same street she had crossed over in her car only minutes before.

The rattle of the keys in her hand against the metal railing reminded her that there were more opportunities to see these views through the huge glass windows and the patio door of the apartment just behind her.

 She opened the exterior door and walked into the spacious main lounge to be met by leather furniture, patterned drapes and cushions, a warm carpet and walls in a salmon colour framing the pictures that must, indeed, be the work of Lawren Drake. This was, clearly, the apartment owned by Jeanette's friend, Anna Drake. Quickly walking from the lounge to the two bedrooms she was delighted with the colour schemes and the ensuite facilities. Both rooms had twin beds, and dressing tables with drawers, and the washrooms had tall clothes cupboards with space above for luggage storage. Last of all, she inspected the kitchen, situated at the back wall of the lounge space and separated from the dining table by a countertop which could be closed off from the lounge by a set of folding doors when the microwave, dishwasher or washing machine were running.

She did not stop to check the contents of the cupboards. Obviously, nothing had been left to chance. Anna Drake had chosen an excellent place in which to relax with friends or to rent out when she was elsewhere. She sent a prayer of thanks winging upward to Anna for such a perfect holiday location.

There were three television sets and a gas fire set into a corner but Valerie could not imagine spending any time watching any of these when a view like this one was available from each of the rooms.

She stepped outside again and as she stood there, she could feel tension flow out of her. She had not been conscious of holding the tension inside, but now that the place had proved to be all she had hoped, her other hopes came to the forefront. This week might, after all, be worth the planning and scheming she had set in motion. Here, she might revitalize friendships and re-establish connections once so important to her. This could be the beginning of the new life she had longed for in the lonely months after David had gone.

There was only one thing missing; the company of Sandra and Corinne.

*

Darkness arrives late on summer evenings in the Lake District.

When dusk was approaching, Valerie sat down with a tray of tea and treats. From the bags of groceries she had purchased in Ambleside, she extracted crisps, chocolate biscuits, Dairylea cheese and fresh granary rolls; all things she could not obtain in Canada.

She was not certain when her friends would arrive. Both were coming by train; Sandra from the north and Corinne from the south. Valerie had advised them to take trains then a taxi from the train station as there was only one parking space available to them in the complex. Valerie thought this would also serve to ensure they spent as much time as possible together when exploring the sights of the area.

The sunset drew her out to the balcony again. The rosy light illuminated the craggy rocks on the summit ahead of her as the rest of the scene dropped into darkness. She was standing there smiling happily when a voice from somewhere below called up.

"Valerie Westwood! Is that you? How do I get up there?"

The voice struck a place in her heart and she knew at once it must be Sandra.

"Sandy! I was just thinking about you. When did you arrive?"

"The taxi dropped me off on a steep road but there was no one around to ask for directions. I've been wandering around up and down flights of stairs trying to find you. This place is built into a hillside, you know. I'm all out of puff already."

"Stay right there! I'll be down to get you. Don't move a muscle!"

In the last light of the day, Valerie ran down the nearest outside stairs with a huge smile on her face. Her heart was beating to the speed of her steps. Sandra! Sandra! Sandra!

She rounded a high hedge and barreled into her friend who was standing on the path on the other side.

They collapsed in giggles and for a moment it was as if all the years had disappeared and they were together in the college room they had shared during so many momentous events.

"Where's your luggage?"

"I left it at the top of the stairs somewhere but please show me where I can sit down before I drop."

"Follow me, then. Our place is just above us. You won't see it at its best until morning but you will love it, Sandy. I am so happy to see you, my dear girl!"

"No one calls me a girl anymore. A girl could run up these stairs without gasping. I think."

"Take your time. We have a whole week ahead of us. A whole week! I'll show you the apartment and then find your luggage for you."

Valerie was glad she had checked out the ups and downs of the complex earlier. Even in the semi dark she knew how to reach the road level and there she spied a white case in front of the office, which was now closed. The thought occurred to her that Sandra might not be the only one who found the complex confusing. What if Corinne had arrived and left again after being unable to track down the right apartment? She fumbled in the pocket of her jacket for her cell phone and checked for text or phone messages. Nothing new. Perhaps Corinne was delayed and meant to arrive tomorrow.

She hefted Sandra's case and decided to return to the road every half hour until it was too late to expect Corinne's taxi to appear. For now, she could not wait to see Sandra's reaction to the apartment. She hoped her guest would have discovered the tray with the teapot and helped herself.

The patio door was still open and lights were on in the bedrooms but no Sandra could be seen.

Valerie hesitated to call out her name. She was probably in one of the washrooms. She looked into the nearest bedroom to see if the washroom door was closed and found her friend huddled under the duvet, snoring lightly. Her shoes were by the bed and an assortment of clothes was scattered on top.

She must be sleeping in her underwear. Poor dear!

She truly was exhausted, by the looks of it.

Valerie's cases were in the bedroom on the opposite side of the apartment. She would not need to disturb Sandra but she couldn't deny her disappointment at being cheated of the chance to spend time alone with her and share her feelings.

"Never mind!" she whispered, as she tiptoed around clicking off lights and closing the double doors that divided the bedrooms from the spacious lounge.

"Everything will be different tomorrow. I can wait. What's one more night after all these years?"

She was no sooner approaching the patio doors to shut the drapes against the night when the phone in her pocket began to buzz.

A new message from Corinne.

> Missed train. Arriving 2morO. Sorry.

"That's short and not so sweet! Oh, dear! Is this a bad omen? Today was going so well. The apartment is stunning, the weather has been excellent, I have plenty of food and a whole program of interesting choices. Have I overdone it? Was the anticipation getting in the way of my common sense? Sandra and Corinne have busy, complicated lives to deal with. I am the one who's free of responsibilities and I have been acting as if they were in the same position. I need to scale down my expectations and take it slowly before I ruin everything for them as well as for myself."

With this sermon running on a loop in her mind, Valerie retired to her bedroom, did some more unpacking and promised herself that the morning would bring a new day and a new improved attitude.

Eight.

<u>Sunday.</u>

Valerie jumped out of bed as soon as she opened her eyes. She was determined to get the day off to a great start and that meant spending time with Sandra.

There was no sign of her friend so Valerie let her sleep and prepared breakfast for them. By the time she had coffee going, toast at the ready and a bowl of eggs and milk sitting by a warmed pan, the sun was well up and supplying another irresistible view from the balcony. She could not wait for Sandra to see it. She tiptoed into the other bedroom with a coffee in hand.

Sandra was not sleeping. She was sitting up in bed crying her eyes out.

"What's wrong? What's happened? Why didn't you come and get me? Sandy! Answer me!"

A swollen face turned toward her and a hoarse

voice squeaked out the words, "Nothing! It's nothing!"

"I don't believe that for one minute! You can't fool me. You know you never could. Fess up!"

At the sound of the old, familiar phrase, Sandra rolled out of the covers and fell into Valerie's arms.

"I am being stupid, that's all. I am so glad to be here but I wasted the evening by falling asleep and now I've made you angry."

"Sandy, the only thing that could make me angry is if you don't explain what's really going on here.

Take a sip of this coffee and calm down."

It felt as if the intervening years had vanished. Valerie had assumed her old role of stalwart support whenever Sandra threatened to fall apart. Only, this time, the friends were no longer teenagers facing their first real challenges but mature women with grown families who depended on them.

"The doctor said it's a mild depression." She stopped to gulp coffee and scrub her face with her free hand. "I have been looking forward to this week. I think I overexerted myself with housework to get everything ready to leave and then I didn't have time to get my hair done and a facial to perk me up and then I couldn't find the apartment and now I've ruined this skirt by sleeping in it and............."

"Stop right there! I won't listen to another word until you jump into that shower. I'll unpack your case and we'll have breakfast out on the balcony together. Believe me, the view out there would make anyone forget their troubles and feel glad to be alive! Go!"

Sandra finally emerged wearing a pair of loose pants and a warm jumper and an apologetic expression. Before she could say anything, Valerie told her to sit and eat while the eggs were hot. She cleared the plate quickly and munched on hot buttered toast while she took in the amazing view. As each minute went by, the sun illuminated a lower aspect of the scene before them. It was like seeing nature revealed in increments so as to highlight its splendour for the very first time.

"Look there!" exclaimed Sandra, rising to lean against the balcony railing for a closer look, "A little white house high up near the woods and there's a road through the field that leads to it. I see a tiny red post office van slowly climbing up the road. Oh, Valerie! This is wonderful!"

Valerie sat back with a satisfied smile. The tears

were forgotten. This was a fresh start.

"What does it make you think of?"

Sandra still gazed out at the hills and finally said, "I suppose I am thinking of the life I lived on Mull before we went to Glasgow. I miss the mountains and the wild sea, the call of the birds and the rivers rushing down the hillsides. It's not really like this scene at all but it reminds me of things that used to be."

"Is that what has been bothering you, Sandy dear?"

"Why am *I* complaining? You've been through so much more than I have lately, Val.
I do miss you though. Why do our lives have to be different from the dreams we had long ago?"

Valerie rose to stand behind her friend at the railing. "I can't answer that question other than to say I have learned lately that we need to cherish each moment whether it matches our dreams or not."

Sandra turned and they hugged.

"You have always been so wise, Val."

"You wouldn't say that if you had seen me a few months ago. I was a total mess!"

The crisis was over and the two old friends fell into the easy companionship they had shared over the years. Valerie described the dark months after David had died and Sandra explained her frustration over her lack of meaningful work. "I am wasting my life, Val, and I don't know what to do about it."

"Put it all aside for now. I can't promise anything but this week is about sharing and remembering and having a darn good time together. There's such a lot to see and do in the Lake District and it looks like the weather will hold for us. Let's tidy up and I'll show you the choices I collected for us.

By the way, I got a text from Corinne. She arrives today. She's such a practical person. She'll set us all to rights, I'm sure."

*

They decided to start by exploring the Lakelands complex. Sandra was determined not to get lost again.

It was easier to figure out the plan in the daylight when signs at the upper road level indicated what apartments and facilities could be found at the bottom of the stairways. They discovered that Valerie's Fairfield apartment was at the highest level, overlooking the manicured gardens and paths. They went into the pool building below the apartment and saw an excellent facility with huge glass windows at the front.

"I am going to swim there, looking out at that view," Valerie insisted.

"Good for you, but I am out of here before I melt. This place is like a sauna!"

The roadway, where all the residents' cars had designated parking spaces, ended at a very steep lane leading down to the streets of Ambleside. Sandra was all for setting off downward until Valerie reminded her she would have to climb up again and they might miss Corinne's arrival while they were in the town.

Instead, they turned around in a circle and revelled in the amazing views from every angle. Valerie mentioned they would get even better views from further up the hillside where houses could be seen bordering a winding street.

"Do you remember the climb up the muddy slope behind the college to get to our residence?"

"Yes! It was a shortcut from the bus stop but dark and dangerous, I suppose. We were brave and bold in those days, weren't we?"

"Some might say more foolhardy than brave.

We could have been attacked there. Grace warned us to stop, didn't she?"

"You're right. She was always watching out for us. I still can't believe she's gone."

Valerie thought it was time to change the subject before Sandra got morose.

"I have an idea. One of us at a time can go down that steep lane and explore the town for a bit. I had a look around yesterday. You go, Sandy. Take your time. There's no rush. Have a bite of lunch if you like. Or bring something back if you want. Take a sniff at the Apple Pie Bakery for example!"

Sandra chuckled, agreed to this plan, and set off slowly on the steep path with a cheery wave.

Valerie went back to the apartment and did some tidying. She intended to move into the bedroom with Sandra and leave the other bedroom for Corinne. She and Sandra had shared a room before and were well used to each other's preferences for dark sleeping conditions and bathroom etiquette.

She finished smoothing the bed she had slept in and wiped the bathroom countertops and sink then transferred her belongings to Sandra's room. Looking around the apartment, she thought it was the perfect place to spend time with friends. The setting was lovely and that view! She was drawn out to see what else was happening. It was like having a giant screen with an ever-changing panorama set in place just for her delight. In the late afternoon the streets far below the Lakelands complex were a hive of activity and all was hustle and bustle. The noise of cars was a background buzz but it was possible to see figures stepping into shops and emerging with purchases or ice creams and wandering along at their leisure.

The day continued warm and the town was busy with weekend visitors. Valerie was lost in a reverie of former days when she and David had strolled along these same, unchanged, narrow streets together, hand in hand, exclaiming at the variety of hand-made chocolates on display or planning their next meal.

She must have been dreaming for an hour or more, or perhaps she was dozing. The sound of a doorbell brought her back, abruptly, to the present. How long had the bell been ringing? It must be Corinne at last.

She rushed to the door at the back of the apartment, thinking Corinne must have seen the sign at the car park that indicated Apartment C could be reached from inside the building. She threw open the door with Corinne's name on her lips but the words died quickly.

This was not Corinne Carstairs.

The young person who stood there was so different from Corinne in every way that Valerie was stunned into silence.

"Excuse me! I am looking for Valerie Westwood. The office people sent me here. It's been a long time but .... aren't you Valerie?"

A thousand thoughts flooded Valerie's mind. This gorgeous creature could only be the girl she had last seen weeping at her mother's grave, and yet, the resemblance was only superficial. She had the elegance and polish of one of those willowy models who grace the pages of high-class women's magazines. From the top of her shiny black hair to the tips of her high-heeled white shoes, she was a symphony in black and white. Her suit skirt was white with dark panels on either side making her body appear ridiculously slender and the white blouse she wore had a dramatic diagonal stripe of black that narrowed towards her tiny waistline.

The effect was both stunning and fashionable.

Valerie absorbed this vision and gulped. She felt the urgent desire to push back her own floppy hair and straighten her shoulders before replying.

"Zoe! How wonderful! I was not expecting you. I hope you haven't been waiting too long. Forgive me for staring. Please come in."

Zoe Morton took command of the situation as if it was the most natural thing in the world. She lifted her black leather valise and marched into the lounge, taking in the entire room at a glance, then, depositing her handbag on the floor by the nearest chair, settled herself into it with a sigh and the swish of nylon as she crossed her long legs.

"I really don't know why I came. It was a last minute decision. The conference I attended this weekend is not far away and it was something about the good weather that may have prompted me to take a short break. Feel free to throw me out if you wish. It was a foolish impulse."

"No! No! Don't even think of leaving! I am so pleased to see you. I had given up hope you would accept my invitation but I'm more than thrilled you came. I was expecting someone else just now and you caught me by surprise."

"Oh, who else is here?"

"No one else at the moment but my old friend Sandra has arrived and Corinne should be here any time now. Do you remember their names?" She shook her head and a perfectly-cut angel wing of hair descended to cover the side of her face, curving to frame her bottom lip. Valerie could not read her reaction to the question. When Zoe looked up again it was to focus on something else entirely.

"I noticed the artwork as soon as I came in. How did you find this place? The prints on the walls are famous and must be worth thousands."

"I am sorry to say I had no idea of their value until I met someone by chance who knows the owner of this apartment and who told me her name. What do you know about the paintings, Zoe?"

She leaned back in her chair and raised one manicured hand toward the largest painting, a study of a house from an unusual angle. The artist must have been far enough above to look down on the building and still show the walls, windows and the large garden at the rear. What made it notable to Valerie was the sunlight that seemed to be shed by the house casting a warm glow around it and encompassing every tree and stone wall in the composition.

"This one is in the boardroom of my company

in London. The previous CEO was born in Scotland and he said the painting reminded him of old stone buildings on the west coast. He said it must have been a beloved place because it radiated love and contentment. The artist is Lawren Drake, of course."

"That fits in with the information I was told. I believe the apartment is owned by his wife."

"An excellent choice for you. Not the only remarkable thing here, I notice."

Zoe unfolded herself from the chair and walked out to the balcony to admire the view. Valerie let her enjoy it on her own. Interrupting the girl with the questions that were crowding her mind would be crass at such a moment. She seemed tightly wound and not exactly communicative. The glorious scenery could only benefit her.

*

While Zoe was still leaning against the railing, the door from the other side of the balcony sprung open and Sandra entered with a canvas bag in her hand, followed closely by a familiar figure toting a case.

"Look who I found outside! She was just as lost as I was. This place is like a warren!"

Valerie crossed the floor in three steps and folded Corinne into her arms. "You are here! I am so glad you made it, my dear. Come in and sit down. Don't worry about your case."

Sandra was heading to the kitchen with her Apple Pie Bakery purchases and providing a running commentary on her Ambleside expedition.

"What a neat little town and so busy with tourists. It must be very popular. There are so many cafes and interesting shops. I wandered around for ages and finally came back to the start. You were right, Val, about the steep climb back. I had to sit down on the top step to catch my breath and an elderly couple carrying two heavy bags of groceries came marching steadily up the hill and continued on up to another level without a pause in their pace and enough spare breath to wish me a good day! I think I must be very much out of shape, Valerie."

"Oh, that hill is a challenge for anyone who isn't used to it. David and I had to wait close to a week to do it without stopping. And we were much younger then."

There was an awkward pause during which Corinne's thoughts were involved in wanting to ask Valerie about David's final months, but she did not feel the time was right for that difficult conversation.

Sandra, still in the kitchen, was feeling renewed guilt that she had not been available to her friend when she lost her life companion and at the same time she was admiring the fact that Val was now able to talk about happier times with David.

Valerie ignored the pause and remembered her hostess duties. She turned to the patio doors where Zoe was entering from the balcony. She had not noticed the new arrivals until the sound of animated chatter drew her attention. She stopped short, trying to remember what, if anything, she knew about these people and also calculating when she could extricate herself from her impulsive mistake in inserting herself into some kind of old gals' reunion.

"Corinne and Sandra, you remember Zoe, Grace's daughter? She arrived a while ago and I am delighted she decided to join us here."

"Actually, I have never met Grace's daughter but I feel I kind of know her from hearing so much about her from you two." Corinne advanced with her hand outstretched and said "How are you? I am Corinne Carstairs," to a startled Zoe, still poised in the doorway with a perplexed look on her face.

"Oh, I didn't see you there, Zoe!" Sandra bounced out of the kitchen and across the floor and almost pushed Corinne aside in her rush to enfold Zoe in a bear hug that nearly swept the girl off her feet.

She lost her breath for a second and missed the opportunity to take her leave as Sandra was determined to fill the gap with reminiscences about Zoe's early years; a period of which the girl had little memory. Despite herself, she was soon caught up in the stream of happenings she had apparently participated in with Sandra and Valerie when they were all in Glasgow.

"And the time we were babysitting for your parents and Valerie let the kettle boil over and the noise and the steam frightened you so much you screamed for ten minutes on end until we found your panda bear under the couch and you settled down with his paw in your mouth, sobbing all over him. When you finally fell asleep, Val snuck the toy away and washed and dried him so your mother wouldn't suspect how upset you had been."

The three women laughed sympathetically and Zoe, in spite of herself was suddenly soothed by the fact that two of them had known her then. In a life in which there was no longer any person who could tell her about her childhood there was a strange comfort in that knowledge.

Valerie could only imagine that the sophisticated young executive was embarrassed by Sandra's tales. She seemed to be somewhat stunned by the turn of events. Val filled the gap by turning to Sandra and pulling her gently away from Zoe.

"Well, Sandy, what did you find to eat in the town? Our travellers must be hungry by now."

"Wait! Please! I want to treat all of you to a meal as an apology for barging in like this. Where is the nearest hotel?"

Zoe's impulse was genuine and yet, she was secretly planning to escape immediately after the meal without causing any further fuss. She could quickly summon a limo and be on the road back to London before nightfall with this whole weird incident left far behind her.

Valerie's face crinkled up as she considered this generous offer. "There are lots of places to have lunch around here but on Sundays only noisy pubs are open late and hotels don't do evening meals unless you are a resident." She rushed on so as not to disappoint Zoe. "There's plenty to eat here, of course. I shopped yesterday and

Sandra has brought more goodies from town. We could have a picnic-style meal here and catch the sunset from the balcony. I have a bottle or three of a decent wine as well."

She turned to include everyone in her appeal. "What do you say? Shall we eat together and plan what we'll do tomorrow? We can start fresh on Monday after a good night's sleep."

The majority vote won.

Zoe was experiencing an unusual, for her, confusion. Normally she was the one in charge; the decision maker who was never challenged. Suddenly she found herself caught up in something totally unexpected, a group of older females who seemed to know more about her than she did.

She took a deep breath. There were things they could never imagine and things they would never know about her. For one more night she could hold it all together and be gone before they suspected a thing.

Nine.

<u>Monday.</u>

Valerie awoke first. As the one who had done the least amount of travelling lately, she felt refreshed in spite of the excessive wine and food consumption of the previous evening.

On the whole she was pleased with the way things were going. Everyone had arrived safely although she feared Zoe's commitment to a week's stay was fragile at best.

The three original friends were very different in style and manner. It would not be easy to establish consensus for anything including where to spend their leisure time. She determined that today, at least, would be about Zoe. Something from the perusal of the tourist folders and brochures must have been of interest to Zoe. Whatever the girl wanted, would be the agenda for the day if Valerie had anything to say about it.

She tiptoed out of the ensuite bathroom and closed the double doors to the bedroom behind her. Sandra was still fast asleep and Valerie needed a few quiet moments to plan the day. Unexpectedly, the patio window was open slightly and she could see Corinne standing at the railing with only a light dressing gown around her.

Immediately Valerie was struck by the thought that something had happened in the bedroom shared by Zoe and Corinne. Although the younger girl had graciously accepted to share, after consuming a considerable amount of wine, it was clear to her hostess that Zoe was accustomed to private facilities when she travelled. The other factor was the difference in personalities between her and Corinne. The latter was a solid, no-nonsense kind of person whose medical career had taught her to brook no fools. Placing these two females together was a risk Valerie had to take but it could have gone horribly wrong.

"Did you sleep well, Corinne?"

"Only as well as someone who is used to early rising and who has plenty on her mind. Did I disturb you, Valerie?"

"Not at all. I confess to sleeping like a baby

these days, but what is troubling you? Is it Arthur? Anything I can do?"

"I doubt it." She wrapped her arms around her waist as if holding herself together. "It's Carla."

"But I thought she had agreed to look after Arthur while you were away."

"It's not that! I just found out about something she's been up to. We had a terrible row. That was why I missed the train. She has been seeing a man."

"Do you mean she's now divorced from her husband?"

"No. That's the trouble. A letter arrived at the house addressed to C. Carstairs and I opened it without thinking. It was from some guy who met Carla in a bar and tracked down her address through her pals.

He wrote begging her to give him her phone info and pick up their romance where it left off.

I was absolutely furious with her. She's living at home and moping around all day doing nothing to sort out her life after two years of marriage. *Two damn years, Val!* That's barely enough time to open all the wedding presents she was given, never mind decide to dump a fellow she promised to love forever.

I tell you, I could have smacked her hard. It's a

good thing I had to leave when I did."
Valerie could see the stress all through Corinne's body. This was not good. Something had to be done to defray the tension.

"Look, it's cold out here. Let me get you the spare comforter and pillows from the closet then you can sit here and watch the sunrise while I make a big pot of tea for us. It's an amazing view."

Valerie popped bread in the toaster while the water boiled and filled a tray with cups, sugar, milk and both butter and marmalade. She kept an eye on Corinne as she worked and noticed she had settled herself in a chair with the comforter around her like a layer of protection from the assaults of her ungrateful child.

It was still early enough to ensure there would be no interruptions from the remaining sleepers as long as they spoke quietly. Valerie closed the glass door behind her when she had deposited the tray. She had no idea what advice to offer about Corinne's situation. It was a dilemma that only the participants could resolve.

"Thank you for this, Val. I feel better just getting it off my chest. I won't burden you any further. Let's eat and watch the sunrise. It looks like another beautiful day."

"Fine with me for now, but know that I won't forget what you have confided in me, Corinne. I want to make this week significant for all of us."

Corinne summoned a smile and bit into a slice of toast dripping with butter and marmalade. As soon as she had swallowed a gulp of steaming tea she asked what Valerie thought about the mysterious Zoe.

Ah, a welcome change of focus, thought Valerie.

"Why mysterious?"

"Well, she's not your average woman. She looks fabulous for one thing. She spent ten minutes in the bathroom last night and emerged wearing a sexy, black silk nightdress. Her skin was shining with health even after she drank most of the wine. I could tell her eyebrows were shaped and possibly tattooed, like the perfect line on her upper eyelids."

"How on earth did you figure that out, Corinne?"

"If you had prepared as many patients for surgery as I have, you would know all the makeup tricks of the trade. You hide something from an anaesthetist at your peril."

"She is a beautiful girl, of course. She has a look of her mother Grace."

"That's as may be, but how did she do this? She has only the briefcase thing and a handbag with her. Where did it all come from?"

"A good question, I think. It's unlikely she has a change of clothes. I hope she won't feel out of place with today's plans. I really want her to stay around for a few days. Did she happen to say anything to you about that?"

"Not directly. We are strangers after all, but I can tell you she spent some time on her smart phone sending out messages. I could hear the tick tick sound of her nails on the screen while I was pretending to be asleep. Oh, there might be one clue about her intentions. I saw that long pamphlet on her bedside table. You know the one with the picture of a house on the cover? She might be interested in that."

"That's good news, for sure. Is there more tea in that pot? I think I'll take a cup in to Sandy and see what she thinks of a visit to Blackwell today. You enjoy the view, my friend. Don't rush."

*

Rushing was the last thing on Corinne Carstairs' mind. She felt as if she had been rushing for years now. Rush to work; rush back home; rush to the shops; rush to feed Arthur; rush to work and the whole cycle began again.

She sat back and took a long, deep breath of the crisp morning air. It tasted like a cold, white wine and she could sense the air filling her body with unexpected energy and, perhaps, just a hint of hope.

This Lake District air was a vast improvement on the overheated, dry air of the hospital. In there, it was either tainted with evil smells, or fraught with fear and anxiety. No wonder she was exhausted at the end of her shift. Fresh, cool air like this would improve results for both staff and patients.

She made up her mind to try to relax and enjoy this mini holiday. She was lucky to have the chance and Val was so kind and almost motherly. Obviously it mattered to her hostess that everyone had a good time. After all, what could Corinne actually do about the hospital situation or about Carla's issues? Part of her was also concerned about Arthur's recovery and what it meant for their future.

It was good to be so far away from her troubles for a change. She would be stupid to waste this golden opportunity.

The sun was rising and shedding a bright glow over the hilltops ahead of her. It was strange to realize that she had nothing demanding her attention at that very moment. This thought was, in itself, a minor miracle. The stiff back which held most of Corinne's tension began to ease as she contemplated a day in which she need make no decisions of any importance. She could feel the crease between her eyebrows relaxing and something was happening to her brain. Is this what it feels like to let go?

Suddenly, it was all too much for her. Tears began to fall on the comforter but she let them flow. Everyone said tears were healing. She had said it herself to plenty of her patients and yet, it was an age since she had cried. As long as no one was watching she could allow this weakness to soothe her weary heart for a moment or two.

*

Sandra had finished her tea while Valerie had a quick shower and dressed in casual clothes for the day.

She could see Corinne huddled inside a cozy comforter on the balcony chair but there was no sign of Zoe. She wondered if the girl had left early. She seemed uncertain of her plans the night before. Even several glasses of wine had not made her more forthcoming.

As she waited to take her turn in the bathroom, Sandra puzzled about Grace's daughter. As a regular reader of women's magazines, she knew about the cosmetic line sponsored by Zoe's company. It was a luxury product far above the level of the inexpensive items Sandra and her daughters bought from the local pharmacy. The ads in the magazines were showcases for the latest young starlet or model with immaculate skin and pouting lips.

Even Sandra could see that their perfection owed little to the cosmetics that were touted in the ads. And yet, thousands of women must buy those products or Zoe would not be the famous CEO of a successful London company, a position she must have earned at a very early age.

Sandra had once read a magazine interview all about Zoe. It was headed in bold print;

Female Exec Helms Excelsior

The interviewer was impressed by Zoe's rise to the top but had concluded, a little reluctantly, it seemed to Sandra, that her position was well deserved. The sentence that lingered in her memory was the one in which Zoe claimed her sacrifices were all worth it. "The climb to the top is damn hard and no one will take it away from me."

The person who had made that statement, was now far from her office and Sandra was finding it difficult to imagine why. Surely, she must be anxious to return to the glamorous, high-powered life of an executive? What could possibly be holding her here with this assortment of older women, none of whom was exactly high-maintenance?

Valerie was standing in the kitchen wondering what her chances were of keeping Zoe Morton in the Lake District for another day when a loud hammering at the apartment door startled her. She jumped, and ran to the door with a sense of déjà vu that only deepened when she saw who was outside with a huge box in her arms.

"Really! Those office people need to up their game. No one could bring this delivery to me. I have had to haul this weight over here by myself!"

She staggered inside, teetering in her sky-high heels and relinquished her burden to Valerie who thought it wasn't all that heavy after all. Perhaps Zoe was not used to hefting anything more weighty than a wine glass these days.

"How did this get here so early on a Monday, Zoe?"

"Oh, I have a 24 hour contract with an express delivery company. I contacted Suzanne last night, she put it all together for me and sent it on. I have been tracking the parcel on my phone but I presumed it would come right to the door."

She sank down on the nearest chair and eased the shoes from her long elegant feet with a sigh.

Valerie was dying to ask what was so important that Zoe had to have it immediately. Something warned her not to intrude, so she poured a cup of coffee for Zoe and sat down to wait.

Her patience paid off when Zoe asked for the kitchen scissors and ripped open the box, extracting a smaller one which she put aside, and then pulling out a collection of casual clothing and shoes all in her signature colours of white and black. There were wedge shoes that laced to the ankle with open space for toes at the front and flat loafers with a white leather tongue. Beside these was a pair of light canvas boots in a tiny dot pattern that Valerie immediately wanted to try on.

There was one pretty white lace sundress with small black daisies sprinkled over it but the rest of the items now heaped on the dining table ranged from an A-line skirt with a front pleat in a houndstooth check with matching vest, to a selection of beautiful trousers and knitwear. It looked as if a fashion show had disgorged its items onto an apartment couch, all at once. Valerie marvelled that such a limited colour palette could produce so many interesting pieces.

Last of all came a pair of jackets for outerwear. One was in butter-soft white leather with black collar and buttons and the other was a rainproof, knee length, hooded overcoat in white with a fine vertical dark line through the fabric that Valerie knew was perfect for the cold or rainy weather that sometimes arrived over the mountains. She found herself bereft of a comment when faced with such luxury but she did wonder who this employee Suzanne was and how she knew exactly the right things to pack on a Sunday when she should be off duty.

The sounds of tissue paper being unwrapped drew Corinne from the balcony and Sandra from the bedroom. The two women were not as reluctant as Valerie to comment on the display.

"Where did you buy this?' asked Corinne, carefully holding up a fine-wool cardigan adorned with diamond-shaped panels gleaming with what looked like Swarovski crystals.

"I shop online sometimes and that piece was from a new collection by A Plus, the hand-made knitwear company operated by the same lady who owns this apartment."

Corinne glanced at Valerie for confirmation and received a nod and a raised eyebrow. She was thinking she must find out more about this intriguing Anna Drake whose name kept cropping up.

"But everything is such a small size," complained Sandra. "People like me can't fit into lovely things like these and we never seem to see them in bigger sizes."

"It's all about knowing where to shop," suggested Zoe, with a smile on her face for the first time.

"And it's about using colour to shape your frame. Anyone can do it!"

Sandra did not look convinced. She was reluctant to touch the clothes the others were exclaiming over. Finding flattering styles was one of her problem issues. She hardly ever shopped for herself these days.

Valerie stood back for a moment and saw two things happening.

First, the interactions among her guests were normal and comfortable for the first time as they shared common interests.

Second, she figured that Zoe had intentions of staying around for a while or she would not have asked for so many clothes. Both revelations brought satisfaction to Valerie and she decided to capitalize on this at once.

"Right, everyone! Get dressed for a day of adventure. You have 15 minutes to get ready. We'll have lunch and dinner out today. Go!

The three voices were raised in surprised laughter at this statement. Even Zoe could recognize a teacher tone when she heard it. There was a flurry of activity as all four scattered to prepare for, they knew not what.

*

It needed twenty minutes in the end but Valerie was able to hustle her group out to the car and get them settled without revealing their destination. She drove to the right out of the complex, down the narrow, winding driveway, made a sharp left onto The Old Lake Road and carefully negotiated her way past, and between, vehicles parked here and there, emerging onto the new highway and heading for Waterhead.

"That was scary!" exclaimed Sandra, once they were safely moving in a straight line.

Valerie felt the same way but wisely concealed the fact. It had been easier to be a passenger on the useful shortcut when David had been the driver, but those days were gone and now it was up to her to make things work.

In a few moments they were in the parking lot at Waterhead and lined up for the steamer which would take them down the whole length of upper Lake Windermere to Bowness at the foot of the tourist town of Windermere.

It was looking like a good day for sailing. No powerful winds to ruffle the surface of the deep blue waters. They chose to stay on the top deck with most of the other passengers, including dogs and children. Valerie shared the excitement of her companions as they compared notes about how long it had been since they had sailed on such a small vessel.

The wind picked up as they struck out for the centre of the lake. Sandra produced a headscarf from her handbag and tied it securely under her chin but Zoe walked the few steps to the teak-topped rail and leaned out into the wind letting the air sweep her shining hair back from her forehead. She stayed there while the announcements alerted the passengers to the history of the lake and the interesting sites they were passing on either side. Their vessel, The Swan, was one of a fleet of boats plying these waters since 1848 and part of a traditional access to a large variety of tour options. Valerie wondered which of the advertised tours might attract her group. The Sunset cruise or the Buffet cruise or any of the shorter ferry rides could take them to a destination.

Some careful navigating through docked sailing ships signalled their arrival at the busy Bowness pier. They disembarked but Valerie led them away from the fair-like atmosphere to the nearby bus stops where she scanned the waiting buses for their next target.

"Do we need a bus, Valerie? It would be faster by taxi."

"Most taxis are pre-ordered here, Zoe. You won't find any empty ones passing by. It's not like London."

"I think I can fix that."

Zoe pulled out her smartphone and pressed a

space or two. Within a few seconds she informed the group that a taxi would be available in exactly one minute at their location.

"How did you do that?"

"Oh, I have an app that connects me to the nearest free taxi and I have already paid the driver."

"Wonderful!" exclaimed the women as they settled into their seats in the capacious car and Valerie told the driver their destination, sending a smile directly to Zoe as she did so and seeing a pleased look on the girl's face.

*

Blackwell House did not look too prepossessing from the road.

As Valerie knew, they were looking at it end on. The house stretched away from them toward Lake Windermere in the distance.

"Come this way before we enter," she insisted. They walked a few steps and turned a corner to see an elaborate façade sprinkled with windows at different levels. The exterior was painted a stark white which glittered in the sunlight.

It was a moment or two before the unusual nature of the structure could be absorbed, then questions started to come.

"Why Blackwell? It couldn't be whiter!"

"How did you find this beautiful house, Val?"

"Can we go in through this part where the stairs are?"

"Isn't this intriguing? Look at the roof line!"

Valerie smiled as her friends began to sound like a class of schoolchildren. "I don't have all the answers but I am not your tour guide today. I suggest we go inside where the tea room and the gift shop are. You can pick up information about the house there. I want you to wander around on your own and choose a spot that speaks to you, where you can sit and think. We'll reassemble at noon in the tea room to order our meals and we'll decide then where we want to eat them. Read the menu board while I get tickets."

She was off before anyone could object.

Corinne walked the length of the house to the sturdy stone wall bordering the lawn and gazed out at the long view across fields to the lake. She thought Zoe was right behind her, but when she glanced back at the elegant figure in a black linen dress with short-sleeved white jacket trimmed in black and sensible flat shoes on her feet, she saw she had not moved.

Zoe studied the styles and placements of the windows and noticed several unique features, deducing that the architect must be a free thinker. She wanted to know more.

Sandra headed for the tea room, as instructed, and planned her meal. She was not as interested in the house tour and thought a delicious lunch would make up for the rather boring part of the day.

Valerie had looked over the pamphlet and thought she knew a bit about Blackwell. She quickly discovered how wrong she was. The wide corridor leading from the gift shop, once the servants' quarters, was such a contrast to the house's exterior that it was as if her sight was dimmed. The dark panelled walls and wooden floor absorbed the feeble light from recessed electric fixtures and her eyes were drawn at once to a bright area at the far end. Before she could reach it, however, an open doorway to her left revealed an extraordinary room best described as a medieval hall. It was impossible to pass by without exploring further.

Several visitors were walking around the huge room exclaiming as they went and Valerie stood just inside the entrance watching them. It was hard to focus on any one feature as the space was filled with unexpected items around the walls, leaving the wooden floor largely bare of furniture.

Where to go first?

There were not one, but two, massive fireplaces. The one to her right was a deep-set inglenook fireplace. As soon as the word 'nook' occurred to her she noticed the room was full of these cozy nooks and she set out to investigate. Close to the inglenook was a piano, set perfectly in a small space between the staircase and the wall. On the other side of this fireplace was a projecting bay window with seat cushions just begging to be used. She began to head in that direction when she saw another padded bench tucked into the left wall. This one was almost private as it was framed on top by a most spectacular ceramic frieze. She had to look closer. The colourful frieze had peacocks with trailing tails and heads turned toward the other fireplace. She estimated that the peacocks might be painted on embossed paper rather than on ceramic tiles but either way, they were gorgeous.

Valerie hesitated. She did not see any signs warning it was not permitted to sit. She could see other visitors chatting on a bench nearby.

She stepped up to the peacock bench and sat, leaning against a section of carved panelling. At once she noticed she was looking at the window exit she had seen from the outside of the house and that informed her this whole baronial room was occupying most of the exterior wall and explained why she had noticed windows at different heights. There were so many large and small windows tucked away in this room. Altogether it was completely original with decorative elements everywhere including a Tudor-style wall effect that started at about head height and continued up to the high ceilings.

The purpose of the room was not clear. Valerie decided it must be intended for many purposes. It was certainly large enough for a ballroom, if needed. The overall effect was not as soothing as she had wanted so she moved to an adjoining room on her left, past the exit door to the side lawn.

This was set up as a dining room on a much smaller scale but highly decorated in a colour theme of blue and purple.

She smiled. Her outfit consisted of a blue jacket and trouser suit over a patterned top in shades of purple. This was obviously the place she was meant to be. Even the fireplace, again a major feature in the room with blue and white delft tiles and the usual fireside seats, had a stone lintel with alternating grey and lilac stones.

Valerie chose a seat near the window so she could see the entire room. It was quiet. The voices from the larger room were hushed. There was a lone bee buzzing against the window trying to escape.

Suddenly the sound thrust her back to the time when David was occupying the dining room at their home with his hospital bed and all the equipment he needed to keep his remaining months tolerable. It was a difficult memory to revisit but she knew she had ignored that memory for too long. Here in this far-away place, she could finally, safely, feel what had been concealed.

*

Sandra left Zoe in the gift shop looking at books about the house, and entered the long, dark hall. She immediately felt the atmosphere there was claustrophobic so she walked quickly to the far end where there was some kind of bright light coming in.

She found herself in a white room. The light

from large windows bounced around so that her eyes needed a moment to adjust. There were a few touches of colour from books on matching shelves on either side of the fireplace and a kind of display cabinet right above the fireplace, but the overwhelming sensation was one of purity and peace. Sandra sank down on the cushioned seats and breathed a sigh of relief. The room was perfect. The kind of room a mother of three active children could only dream of.

Each item was placed in exactly the right position and no one would ever dare to move a single thing.

She laughed out loud when she noticed the delicate white-painted wooden columns projecting from the walls had small inserts of mirror so that sunlight shone into her eyes. Even on a dull day, she thought, this room would be bright and cheerful. It really demanded a special outfit to match. She tugged self-consciously at her faded green skirt and old beige cardigan. She could not imagine why she was alone in these beautiful surroundings. Surely others would soon discover this treasure but she decided to relax for now and look out of the window at the lawn and the far view across fields to the lake.

She was almost drifting off when the sound of children's voices startled her. Out on the lawn in the sunlight four children were chasing each other around to the kind of screaming laughter that is universal when children run free. A wave of emotion swept over her and it was a second or two before she could identify its source; she was feeling homesick for her grandchildren! Of course it was Monday, one of the days when the littlest ones came to spend the day so her daughter could work. Had she wedded herself so closely to this part of her weekly routine that the absence affected her when she was supposed to be on holiday?

She watched the children play and wiped a tear from her cheek. She would stay here, thinking, until another visitor arrived in the white room to claim her place.

*

With the Blackwell guide book in hand, Zoe followed the floor plan. It was her intention to approach the interior in her usual methodical way, but after reading that Blackwell House was designed by Arts and Crafts architect Mackay Hugh Baillie-Scott and featured 'a treasure trove of handicraft, carvings, stained glass, metalwork, textiles and furniture' she was intrigued enough to abandon her initial approach and seek out the unusual aspects. She puzzled about something listed as a Minstrel's Gallery. What could that represent in an early twentieth-century house? She set out to find it and was stunned by the dimensions of what was described as the Main Hall. Its proportions and intricate decorations were overwhelming.

What kind of family would require such a room in the centre of their home?

Quickly bypassing a monster of a fireplace, she escaped by way of a set of stairs to the Minstrel's Gallery from where she had an elevated view of the huge room below. So, the idea was medieval. All it lacked was a small orchestra of players to entertain the guests in the fashion of a royal castle's Great Hall. Truly, it was a mishmash of styles without a clear focus. The predominance of dark wood everywhere was depressing.

To her right was a small bay window looking out on the bright garden view at the side of the house where Valerie had first taken them. She moved there to escape the gloomy atmosphere surrounding her and wondered why she had been so affected by it. Accustomed to analysis of motives in her business world she applied the same mental discipline and soon came up with a startling reason. In a strange way this vast, empty space below her reminded her of her own London apartment .

But why? The two could not have been more different in style. Hers was a loft space, originally a warehouse converted to high-priced industrial apartments. It was lit by enormous windows reaching to the ten-foot ceilings and was minimalist in décor from its polished concrete floor to the white and grey modern furnishings. The granite countertops and seldom- used stainless steel appliances repeated the monochrome theme. Where her living space was at one extreme of a spectrum; the main hall below was at the other.

Was that why the comparison had sprung to mind? Did it mean that each style was equally insufficient? Did it matter? Hers was a twenty-first century apartment and she hardly spent any time there. She had given the job of decorating to a fashionable modern stylist and changed nothing since then. Perhaps that was the problem. There was little in her living space that declared the interests of the owner. She had never taken the time to personalize it. It struck her that she could sell the place tomorrow and, other than her clothes, she would not choose to take anything with her.

This seemed to suggest she was a very boring person. Was there something to be learned in this house?

She knew enough about the Arts and Crafts style to understand the importance its devotees gave to the beauty of every item in a house, no matter how prosaic its uses. Such details as wrought iron door handles and hand-crafted wall coverings, were chosen with the greatest of care. She had once visited Standen, the William Morris house near East Grindstead and there the link to Blackwell was obvious in the tiniest items like candlesticks as well as in the larger furnishings and stained glass.

She began to speculate on what changes she could make to warm up her own living quarters. A touch of colour here and there might be a pleasant addition without causing much disruption to her surroundings.

Zoe sped out of the Ministrel's Gallery and up the shallow steps to the upper level. She was on a mission to find small, telling items which she could adopt for her London apartment. She would take photographs to remind her.

*

Corinne had started the day outdoors and now she felt as if she had spent enough time in her life indoors. On such a glorious day it was a crime to waste it inside any building, no matter how interesting. After peering over the stone wall for a while, she reversed her direction and walked back around the end of Blackwell House with only a brief stop to glance over the chalkboard menu in the tea room.

Whereas the south side of the building was covered in windows, the north was quite plain. The only major feature appeared to be a large double door surmounting a set of stone steps. This door looked like solid oak; the kind of thing you would see in a cathedral perhaps. It was set in a porch that projected out from the building and there were decorated windows to either side. No one seemed to be entering or leaving by this door and Corinne wondered if it was once meant to be the main entrance to the house.

She continued across the gravel area which could have parked a number of cars or carriages but was now hosting visitors wielding glasses of what looked remarkably like wine.

As she walked forward, she came to a stone wall which might have been a continuation of the one on the other side of the house. This wall, however, dropped down about ten feet and enclosed a narrow terrace set with small tables and chairs. She considered this as a location for lunch but dismissed it reluctantly. Despite a very pretty flower display on the wall facing out to the lake, the tables only suited two people and would, at that, be a tight fit.

There was one more possibility. A set of steps led down between the terrace and the wall of the house.

At the ground level she discovered a much longer, wider flagstone terrace with a series of wooden tables and chairs ample in size for four diners and with large umbrellas to shade from the sun, now high overhead. Past the end of the house the terrace was sheltered by the depth of the stone wall buttressed at regular intervals and between the stone buttresses was a garden of summer flowers and trailing or climbing plants where bees buzzed happily and lavender gave out its seductive scent.

"Exactly right! We can all eat here in comfort." Corinne noticed numbers on metal plates set into the centre of each table. She took a minute to wander along the terrace checking out the view across the green lawn toward the lake and hills beyond. She found the perfect table right in the centre, noted the number and left her jean jacket on one of the chairs to claim it.

Far above her, Zoe was gazing out of a bedroom window and spotted Corinne in pale blue jeans and dark short-sleeved top walking purposely along the edge of the lawn. Zoe looked at her watch and realized the time had flown by. If she wanted to join the women for lunch she had better find her way back to the tea room.

*

Sandra was first in the tea room and soon found it necessary to order her meal and find a table. It was a small area and filling up rapidly with pairs of older women who had relatives with them on a day out, and who were determined to reserve their portion of the delectable home-cooked meals on offer for the day. It looked as if some items might be sold out before the others arrived to join her.

She was dithering about ordering for the others, just in case, when Valerie appeared. She had wisely left a pre-order earlier and joined a smaller queue to the side of the counter to collect her food. Returning with a loaded tray, Val assured Sandra she had brought enough for two people at least. Since Sandra had been generous with her own order, they felt secure that the latecomers would not be left out.

Next to arrive was Corinne, looking very pleased with herself. She spotted her friends and told them she had found an ideal spot to eat outside. This idea was quickly accepted as the tea room was not only crowded but also very noisy with chattering females everywhere.

Corinne approached the counter and nabbed a young server who agreed to find someone to carry the trays of food to the designated table and who prepared a separate tray with wine and glasses for Corinne to carry there.

With Corinne leading the way, the trio soon found the location and all exclaimed at the perfect weather and marvellous views. They poured the wine, toasted each other, and settled down for a grand meal to come.

Zoe arrived shortly thereafter with news that tea, coffee and desserts would arrive in due time.

There was immediately a party atmosphere

which continued all through the food consumption and until the last crumbs of the delicious puddings and cakes had been spooned up.

As she looked around at her guests relaxing with full stomachs and contented expressions , Valerie felt hopeful that the moment was right to start on her plan to bind the women closer together.

"So ladies, what was your favourite spot in the house?"

Corinne answered at once with an apology. "I have to confess that I really didn't see the inside of the house. It is such a grand day, I couldn't force myself to go indoors so I have been wandering around outside imagining what it would be like to own such a place in such a spot."

"Well, you get a pass, Corinne, after finding this amazing spot for us to enjoy lunch. Anyone else want to respond?"

Sandra was feeling slightly inebriated and able to speak more freely than she normally would.

"I loved the white room two floors above here. It was the most peaceful place I have been in years and made me think about myself and the things in my life that are really important to me.

I had a long time alone in that fabulous room and I think it has changed me."

No one wanted to push Sandra to describe what she meant by this personal statement.

Zoe took a cue from her and announced, "I know what Sandra means. I had a bit of a change experience at Blackwell. For a start, I love the architectural features. It is a most unusual design incorporating crafts and elaborate detailing. I really should not have liked any of it. My style is modern and minimalist but there was such art in every corner of the place and I think it has made me re-think the decorating elements in my own flat. I might even add a spot of colour here and there."

This revelation caused the others to break into laughter.

"What?"

"Zoe, look at what you are wearing. You don't own anything coloured."

"Other than her red lipstick," added Sandra.

"Now you've introduced the topic, Zoe, why only black and white?"

Zoe had to think about it. She had made the decision years before and now it was like her trademark.

"Well, it began as an answer to a problem. When I started work in the cosmetics industry I found it difficult to keep up with the clothing standards. I had little time to shop as I worked so hard to gain a foothold and I found it easier to have a simple plan. Black and white was the cheapest and most practical scheme I could think of and it worked in all seasons."

Corinne's eyebrows raised as she considered this answer. "I suppose it's no problem to get dressed in the morning. Pretty much everything in your closet matches!"

More laughter met this observation and Zoe joined right in. Of course, they were right!

Valerie felt encouraged by this result and hoped it meant the four women might make a happy group and enjoy the rest of the week together. Even if Zoe left tomorrow, which seemed likely, this time with her had broken down some barriers.

Zoe was totally surprised at her own reactions. She thought she had nothing in common with the group and yet she was actually laughing at herself, with them, and feeling quite good about it. How different this was from her usual, limited interactions with women in the work place. There she was seen as the boss and no one acted normally with her. They were afraid of her power and she was afraid of losing that power.

She stood up and excused herself, walking quickly over the lawn and talking into her phone.

"Have we upset Zoe by laughing at her?" asked Sandra, shocked at the abrupt change of manner.

Valerie watched Zoe's back and suggested she had just been reminded of her business responsibilities and was concerned about keeping in touch. "She isn't used to taking time off, I think."

The others nodded in agreement and talked about other things until Zoe returned.

"Everything all right?" queried Valerie.

"Yes," was the reply. "Suzanne's doing a wonderful job and she says I should stay longer."

Valerie refrained from sounding too enthusiastic about this idea in case she chased Zoe away but she did say she was more than welcome to stay; a sentiment that was echoed by Sandra and Corinne.

"I, for one, need to stretch my legs after that feast," said Valerie. "Who's joining me?"

They took a walk around the property together

and took turns pointing out features gathered from their varied experiences inside. It was decided that Corinne's observation about the site of the original front entrance was correct and Zoe proved it by opening the floor plan she found in the guide book. She was able to fill in a few facts about the history of the house, including that it had been a girls' school for a period and that the Holt family, who had commissioned the house, had not occupied it for very long owing to the death of their only son during the First World War.

The four women were in the taxi heading back to the steamship harbour when Sandra thought to ask if anyone had discovered why the house was named Blackwell. No one had. Amidst more laughter they all decided it was a good excuse to return some day to find out.

*

Much later that evening, Valerie and Sandra had a quiet talk as they prepared for bed.

"It's been such a good day, Val. I can't believe we never thought to do this kind of thing before. It's all thanks to you, of course."

"Don't imagine I'm not getting as much out of

this as every one of you!"

"I know you are, my dear friend, but what a great plan for a day. The return trip on the lake and the great food at the Waterside Restaurant before we headed back here were the perfect finale. Remember how Corinne laughed when she realized we could eat outdoors again? I don't think she has had such a good time in years and, come to think of it, neither have I. I just realized I haven't watched television once since I came here. Now that's a change for me."

Valerie smiled to herself as she thought over her plan for the next day. With any luck, and the weather holding, Sandra Halder would not be watching TV on Tuesday either.

Ten.

<u>Tuesday.</u>

Valerie had to reveal her plan for the day, early in the morning. She knew special clothing would be required and some of it might have to be purchased. The first order of business had to be shopping in Ambleside.
She suspected Sandra, born on a mountainous island, might have brought some suitable outerwear in her case and this proved to be so. The two women provided a fashion show of a kind so the other two would know what they were looking for. Valerie had an old, but valued, Gore-Tex jacket. Its fingertip length, hood, and wind and waterproof fabric, could protect against most weather situations. Sandra's short coat was similar, and even older, but still serviceable.

"Don't spend a lot of money on this unless it fits into your lifestyle," warned Valerie. She knew how costly such items could be. "The best place to spend for value and safety, is on your feet."

She showed her leather boots and pointed out the gripping soles, laces, and ankle support.

Sandra asked if her hefty, all-purpose trainers would suffice and Valerie accepted them with the proviso that she had climbing experience since childhood and that would make the difference.

Two hiking sticks were produced from Valerie's case and expanded to demonstrate how they worked. She was willing to lend one, or both, of these.

"So, exactly what did you two have in mind for today's adventure?" asked Corinne, with some considerable concern on her face.

Zoe, who had been planning to leave for London as soon as she had presented something special she had ordered for the women, figured out it obviously would not be this morning. She, too, wondered what was coming.

"Well, you only have to look out the windows to know this place is not just about lakes. To come here and not experience the mountains would be a crime." Valerie paused, expecting some objections and she was right.

"Hold on, there! I am not a mountaineer. I intend to return home in one piece."

Zoe felt she need not add to Corinne's concerns. It must be quite clear to everyone that she was not familiar with athletic pursuits.

"Now, you know Val would not take us into danger! We had a chat about this last night and Val knows a very easy climb for today. If we all behave and follow directions we may get a chance to do something more ambitious another day." Sandra couldn't keep a straight face as she said this. She knew she was doing a parody of Valerie.

"Do you all trust me? I know what I'm doing." This was said with a sidelong glance at a giggling Sandra.

A chorus of "Yes, Miss!" greeted her and Valerie once again felt encouraged. A group that can laugh together might stay together.

"Off you go, then! As soon as you walk down the steep lane you will see sports outfitters on the main street. There are various price ranges for hiking supplies so don't buy at the first one you see. And remember to try the boots on and walk around in them. The last things you need are blisters. And don't forget to buy thick socks!"

With this caution she dismissed Corinne and Zoe to find equipment and she and Sandra began to discuss what supplies they would need for the day. Valerie had a backpack that would hold bottled water and fast energy snacks like fruit, chocolate and crisps.

"Do we really need food?"

"No one ate this morning after yesterday's indulgence but hiking in the fresh air always gives you an appetite. I have an idea for a good place to eat a late lunch, but this will do for now. Do we have sunscreen and hats?"

A search for these items began. Once they were found, Valerie stepped out onto the balcony and studied the sky. There were more clouds floating along than there had been before. She calculated that the day would likely be fine with less sunshine and a light wind; not a bad thing when climbing. The weather report indicated a change but nothing too unnerving. They should have a good experience. Valerie wanted to provide lasting memories for her friends and she knew how to do that, in this respect, at least.

It was a full hour before Zoe and Corinne returned with their purchases. It appeared they had had a good time shopping as they seemed relaxed together and had helped each other up the steep lane.

Both had walked back with their new boots to break them in and pronounced their footwear "Excellent!"

Zoe decided to wear her own raincoat as it was as good as anything else she had seen in town. Valerie insisted she wore one of her cashmere sweaters underneath for an added layer of warmth. After she had inspected everyone's outfits she proclaimed the expedition ready to go.

The drive from Ambleside to White Moss Common was one of the prettiest in the Lake District. Valerie drove as slowly as she could on the winding road so her passengers could admire the scenery, and there was a lot to admire. As each hill or mountain appeared round a bend, Corinne would ask, "Tell me that's not the one I have to climb." She repeated this line so many times it became a running joke and inevitably brought another laugh.

When they drove into the parking area at White Moss Common there was no mountain in view, only a peaceful riverside where families picnicked and children played in the shallows. Corinne was reassured and Valerie did not tell her anything different. The party of four emerged from the car and piled on their outerwear. Valerie had her Gore-Tex tucked into the straps of her backpack and suggested the coats would not be needed just yet. Sleeves were then tied around waists and the group crossed over the river by a wooden bridge and soon found a wide path rising through a wooded slope.

"This isn't too bad," whispered Corinne to Zoe. "I can do this!"

Zoe did not contradict her but she had spied a tall drystone wall far ahead and suspected there was worse to come. Going through the sheep gate in the wall was a new experience for Corinne and Zoe. The slim young woman slipped through easily while Corinne managed to get herself stuck in the middle for a moment as she negotiated the sheep barrier in the centre.

The next part was a trek uphill on a rough stony track along the boundary wall between the lower levels and the heights. The hiking sticks came into service and some puffing and panting could be heard. This part lasted for several minutes but they soon crested the rise and had their first view of their destination.

They were high enough now that they could see the river below and the shoulder of a mountain to their left. Ahead was a well-defined path leading to a straight line along an earth-packed terrace that curved into the mountainside and was supplied with benches and seats at regular intervals.

There were no comments at first as the climbers took in the scope of the terrain in front of them. They could see the edge of a lake several hundred metres below but the brush-covered slope did not suggest an easy descent that way, while the mountainside to their left rose high enough to blot out most of the sky. A quavering voice asked again, "Please tell me that is not the mountain I have to climb!" and the tension was broken.

Through her laughter, Valerie assured her companions they were not required to scale Silver How as the descent on the other side would lead them miles away and take several hours of serious effort. Instead, they could spend as much time as they wished admiring Grasmere from on high and if anyone wanted to ascend a little way up the mountain for an even better view they were welcome to do so.

Reassured by this, the women marched forward and with each step more of Grasmere Lake came into view. It was a well-known panorama which still had the ability to amaze Valerie each time she saw it. The effect on those seeing it for the first time was quite remarkable.

"It feels Godlike to be able to see so much at one time."

"Those mountains way in the distance must be gigantic! Need I say I don't want to climb *them*."

"The water on Grasmere is as still as a reflecting mirror."

"The people down on the beach below us are so small!"

"I can't believe I feel so safe on this earth path. Yesterday's stone-flagged terrace was flat on the ground and this one is a complete contrast, yet they are both well named."

"Look! The river we crossed at the beginning flows right from this lake."

"I'm going to sit on that bench and take photographs. No one will believe me otherwise."

Sandra bravely ventured up one of the marked paths for about a hundred metres before she turned and scrambled back down announcing she was out of practice and Val was right about the greater height being astonishing. "I'd forgotten that coming down is so much harder than climbing up. I was too shaky to think of taking a picture. Now I feel ravenous. Anyone else ready for a snack?"

No one felt like joining her. It was enough food for the spirit to absorb the sheer beauty of nature surrounding them.

A few serious climbers passed by with a smile and greeting. Most headed up the marked paths to the heights and were soon gone from sight.

Clouds left moving shadows on the scene and birds flew by below the group. An hour passed by without much talk. They were lost in their own thoughts until Valerie spoke again.

"I feel so glad to share this experience with all of you. I can't help thinking of happy times here with David and of dear friends like Grace who never got to see this with me. She would have found so much joy in this peaceful place and ...."

Before Valerie could finish, Zoe sprang up and set off away from the group at a furious pace.

Three heads turned in unison to try to understand what just happened. Valerie came to her senses first and yelled out to Zoe to stop. The girl kept running. Valerie was already on her feet and several yards in pursuit, when she turned to say, "You two please stay right here. If Zoe turns the wrong way at the end of this

terrace she will get well and truly lost."
With mouths open in surprise the two women watched as Valerie ran after Zoe, disappearing through a gate into thick woods on the side of the next mountain.

*

Please, God, let me find her before I run out of steam. I knew something was wrong and this proves it.
She ran at the sound of her mother's name. Why would she do that if there wasn't a reason?
Valerie scanned the woods directly in front of her. The hillside was narrow and fell into a ravine within a few feet from the trail but it also went downhill steeply by the fence so she could see a little further through the thick belt of trees.
A flash of white to my left! She's wearing the white jeans; it's Zoe!
She called her name again but there was no change in the girl's headlong rush downward. A ray of sunlight caught the gleam of that black wing of hair but Valerie knew she had no hope of catching up with the girl when she had to give most of her attention to where her own feet were placed.
If she doesn't slow down soon she will be over the

edge and rolling down a hundred feet into the ravine. Help me, Grace!

Minutes later a cry of pain rang out and the sound of Zoe's feet pounding the undergrowth stopped. Valerie stopped too and listened, breathlessly, to hear if she had tumbled beyond reach. No further noises reassured her that Zoe was no longer moving or falling.

"I'm coming, Zoe! Keep calling until I find you!"

No point in rushing now. Watch your feet, Val. Don't trip, whatever you do. Go slow and listen.

She found the girl curled up against the trunk of a giant evergreen tree. She had tripped over a root and twisted her foot. Valerie prayed it wasn't a broken bone. It would take an hour or two for the mountain rescue team to reach them here and by then shock would have set in. She blamed herself for leaving behind her backpack although it would have been a hazard in these close quarters.

She carefully and gently felt Zoe's foot and ankle. Swelling was obvious already. It was going to be painful but nothing appeared to be broken. The first requirement was to bind up the foot to prevent any more swelling from immobilising Zoe. What could she use? She looked over her own clothing, then Zoe's, but nothing seemed to fit the bill.

Suddenly she remembered the scarf tucked into the back pocket of her blue jeans. It had been there since she packed her clothes in Canada; an old habit from her teen years in Glasgow where it was always advisable to carry a headscarf in case the weather took a turn for the worse. She quickly unwound it and was relieved to find it was one of the long, filmy kinds of scarf. It did not have the weight that was needed but, perhaps, its length would make up for other deficiencies.

Zoe had still not said a word. She allowed Valerie to wind the scarf in layers starting with her foot and working as far up the ankle as the scarf would stretch, knotting it behind with the last spare inch of material.

"I'm so, so sorry, Valerie. I didn't mean to cause this trouble. I am ashamed of myself."

Valerie could hardly hear this whisper. Her mind was working on how to get the girl down the mountain safely. "Hush! my dear wee one", she said, using a phrase from her years with her own young children.

This was not the right thing to say. Zoe collapsed in tears and cried out between sobs,

"My mother used to say that. My mother! I can't hold this in a moment longer. She would want you to know, Valerie. She loved you and Sandra."

"What is it, Zoe? I could tell there was something eating at you. Is this why we lost touch after Grace died?"

"I couldn't face you. I couldn't deal with it. I just ran away like a coward."

"Tell me everything. It will help, I assure you." Huddled together with Valerie's arms around her for warmth and comfort, the shocking story spilled out in a rush.

"My lovely mother committed suicide. She took pills and left me a short note to tell me my father had been having an affair for years. She wrote she could not bear the shame and disappointment so she took her own life.

She left me alone to cope with this. I was totally distraught but I did what I could to control the damage to the family and to my mother's reputation. I disposed of the note and the pill container and cleaned up the sick on her bed. I arranged her body to look as if she had died in her sleep and then called the doctor. I begged him on bended knees to sign the death certificate and declare my mother's death as a heart attack. He was an old man on his last legs who knew the family. He wept with me and did as I asked. He was dead within a year taking the secret with him.

I then went to find my father and told him what I thought of him. I warned him to keep quiet about all I had done. It was the last time I spoke to him, or saw him. He left the house, and my life, that same night."

At Zoe's first words, Valerie had stiffened in shock. She scarcely breathed until the end of the appalling story. This explained so much. Michael Morton had not been present at his wife's funeral. No wonder Zoe was so withdrawn; so unemotional. She could not afford to let down her guard and risk these horrors escaping her control.

The girl looked up at her mother's friend expecting to see her own self-disgust mirrored in the older woman who had been subjected to this confession without warning. Valerie's heart ached for all the pain the young girl had suffered. She gathered Zoe into her arms and promised all would be well. It was over now. It was done. She had chosen the right path for her mother and Grace Morton was in a better place.

She had to repeat this mantra several times before Zoe began to relax the tension keeping her body rigid.

The silence among the old-growth forest trees sent blessings down upon the pair. Gradually their breathing resumed a normal rhythm and Valerie was almost positive the girl was sleeping. She let her thin frame rest among the tree roots and whispered in her ear that she was going to get help and would be back very soon, cautioning her to remain still.

Valerie found her muscles had stiffened during the period of immobility so it took her several steps before she was walking upright again. She faced uphill and trudged as fast as she safely could towards the gate in the fence.

To her relief, on the other side of the gate she met Sandra and Corinne, carrying all their belongings and obviously worried about what had happened to their companions.

"I can't explain it all here but I am *so* glad to see you two. Zoe has twisted her ankle, I think. I'll lead you to her and you can check the bandage, Corinne. It was the best I could manage. Watch your feet as you go down here."

In minutes, Corinne had approved of Valerie's first aid attempts and looked into Zoe's eyes for signs of concussion, declaring her fit to continue downhill with help. They bundled her into her windproof jacket and commandeered two of the hiking poles so she could keep her foot off the ground. Corinne took her weight with an arm under her weaker side and Sandra and Valerie went ahead cautiously, watching out for tripping hazards.

It was slow progress but each step brought them closer to the paved roadway that began halfway down the forested area where a few houses were situated in clearings above the lakeside.

Corinne knocked on the door of the first of these houses and asked for hot tea and an ice pack for the patient. The young woman inside was eager to help and soon had the four seated comfortably on her porch while she fetched tea, a cold pack from her fridge and a bandage from her medicine cabinet.

Corinne unwound the temporary bandage and was happy to declare there would be no lasting damage to Zoe's foot other than some swelling and bruising which would disappear in time.

The casual chatter and competent ministrations soon had Zoe feeling much brighter. She insisted she was fine and would not hear of holding up the day's plans any further.

Corinne made a deal with her. If her boots still fit and she could walk with only the hiking sticks for support until they reached flat ground, they would continue with whatever plan Valerie thought was appropriate.

Zoe looked paler than usual but seemed to have recovered her usual confidence. She managed to meet Corinne's requirements and the quartet soon reached their planned destination, The Gold Rill Hotel where Valerie had stayed for her first night in the Lake District. They settled happily in the comfortable lounge at the stroke of two o'clock and were just in time to order hot lunches delivered to their table.

No one asked Zoe what had happened to cause her accident. It was a sensitive conspiracy of silence among the older women and as soon as the food arrived they were all distracted by the aromas and the promise of what Valerie had described as 'the best sticky toffee pudding you will ever eat!'

Valerie made a short detour to the front desk where she asked for a taxi to deliver them back to the White Moss parking area in an hour or so. When Sandra discovered Val's original plan was to walk through Grasmere Village, and along the road to their starting point, she thanked Zoe for causing the change of plan as she swore she would never have survived that walk in one piece.

*

In high spirits, the party arrived back to base and collapsed onto chairs and couches.
No one had asked what caused Zoe's sudden departure on the mountainside.
It looked as if recovery naps were required until Valerie suggested a better way to relieve any muscle stiffness.
"The swimming pool lies beneath this apartment and we have permission to use its facilities. There's a hot tub and Sandra can attest the temperature in the whole pool area is like a sauna so you won't suffer from cold. Let's go down and relax. We'll leave Zoe here in peace."
Corinne checked that Zoe would keep her foot elevated and alternate the hot and cold treatment that was known to reduce swelling. Corinne had placed a wet, heavy sock in the freezer to act as an ice pack. They left Zoe there with her phone to her ear and the television remote for company.
The three women were soon inside the pool area

changing room and Sandra could wait no longer.

"Did Zoe pledge you to secrecy, Val? I am dying to know what happened on the mountain."

Corinne was curious also but aware she did not have the long association with Zoe's family that was common to the two older women. "Look, I can go down for a swim and leave you to talk privately."

"No! You both deserve an explanation and there's a reason why I want you to hear. I'm going to need your help with Zoe."

They sat on the change room's wooden bench and gave Valerie their full attention. She grasped Sandra's hands tightly, knowing what she had to say would affect her the most. The bare outline of Zoe's sad story was told quickly and both women gasped in shock. Neither could ever have suspected such a grim, dark tale haunted the polished exterior of the girl they had envied.

"Good God! That's horrific! What can we do to help?"

"I just want to take Zoe in my arms and hold her like I did when she was just a bairn. She must have suffered terribly for years. I feel awful that we didn't know anything about this. She has been so alone."

"She's not alone now, Sandy. We can help her if you two will agree to share some of your own stories. I think she's consumed by guilt and we all know enough about that subject to show her she's not the only one. No one gets a get-out-of-jail-free card on that part of life's experiences."
Two heads nodded eagerly. They would do anything if she thought it could help.

"Thank you both sincerely. It's a lot to ask. Let's go down the stairs to the pool and hot tub and prepare for what will be a difficult discussion."

When the trio returned to the apartment, relaxed and soothed from their spa break, they found Zoe sitting on the couch with a determined expression on her face.

"Please sit down, ladies. I need to say some things to you before I go."
Corinne protested. "Look, Zoe, I am glad you feel better but it would be a mistake to put too much weight on your foot for a day or two, and no high heels of course!"

"You are right Nurse Carstairs! I didn't express myself very well. I won't be leaving today but I can't spend another night here without setting the record straight. I boiled some water for tea so we can be civilized. My mother always said tea makes all crises seem better."

Valerie noted this was the first and only time Zoe had mentioned her mother in public. She took it as a good sign and sat down beside her while Sandra went to pour tea and set it on a tray.

In the end no one actually drank any tea. They could not take their eyes off Zoe or miss one word she said in the next half-hour.

"I want to start by saying what it has meant to me to be accepted into this group of friends. I really did not intend to join you here but circumstances led me to you and I am glad from the bottom of my heart.

You didn't know me before but I can assure you I am now utterly different. I don't mean only superficially, although I will do something about the black and white thing very soon. It's inside me that the real change has occurred. I can see now what I have missed by shutting myself away from life.

The pain never lessens when it is continually squashed into smaller and smaller places. It just gets more intense. I suspect this pain was also beginning to affect my business dealings so you have saved me from that disaster too."

She took a deep breath, looked over to Valerie for strength, and continued to speak with her gaze fastened on the carpet at her feet.

"My mother; the dearest, sweetest, most loving, smartest woman in the whole world was driven to such abject despair that she took her own life. She never indicated by word or manner what turmoil she must have been enduring to get to such a place and I feel anguished that I was not more observant and also not at home as much as I could have been. Perhaps I could have saved her. Perhaps not.

This is long years ago now but I have lingering anger; sometimes against my mother, God help me, and also a rage against my father than has never diminished. I blame him for setting all this in motion with his actions. He has never approached me to explain what he did."

The silence in the room was palpable until Zoe raised her eyes in fear to look at her audience. What she saw then, proved to her how right she had been to trust these unknown women with her deepest, most tormenting secrets. Each one of them had tears on her cheeks and, acting as one body, they gathered closer so they could all touch her and convey without words how much support they wanted to give.

Something unlocked in Zoe Morton at that moment. Some things evaporated. Some got lighter and she knew she would never again feel so alone.

There was a lot of murmuring, a lot of dabbing at tears and, finally, a beginning of a conversation Zoe had not expected and would not have known how to ask for.

Valerie nodded to give Corinne the go ahead.

"Listen, my dear girl! You have endured a horrendous shock and loss but I am here to tell you we are all familiar with the guilt and the anger you speak of. In my case, I am guilty of so many offences against my daughter. Some, believe it or not, have begun to become clearer to me in the last few days here with you all. Often, distance from a problem can bring some clarity.

I have shown absolutely no sympathy to Carla in this separation from her husband. I have transferred my own feelings of anger at the amount of patience and effort it has taken to persevere in my own long marriage, onto Carla, blaming her for giving up too soon. I have chastised her like a wayward child instead of listening to her reasons. This latest episode with the 'boyfriend' drove me over the edge and I am ashamed of my behaviour. My only hope is that her father has calmed things down. It wouldn't surprise me if she was gone for good by the time I get home again."

Corinne sat back against the chair and looked out at the darkening sky with a thoughtful gaze.

"Oh, well, if it's true confessions you want, I can volunteer mine!"

All eyes turned on Sandra who was now pacing up and down the space in front of the patio windows ignoring the view of the cloudy sky and the high hills and working herself up into a state where she could express, physically, all that she had kept under wraps. Even Valerie was surprised by her reaction.

"With me, the anger is turned inward and festering away inside me. No, it's not something ghastly like Zoe had to endure. *Nothing* we can say would compare to that, but it's destructive all the same and the worst thing is, I can only blame myself.

I look at Zoe with a career and so many choices in her life. I admire Corinne's devotion to a caring vocation, despite its difficulties. I know

Valerie's lifelong profession has contributed so much to so many children and then I look at myself. What have *I* done with my life?"

"Wait a minute!" interrupted Valerie. "You brought up three lovely daughters and help out with your grandkids. That's not nothing!"

"But what you don't know is the way I am wasting my life. Ian has his work which he loves. He travels often and he has always provided well for us. Could be that's part of the problem. There was no real need for me to teach to help out financially. I sat at home after the girls were all in school and did nothing. No hobbies; no community work; no school volunteering; no real family contacts. Nothing!

Day after day, and month after month; years of nothing! I watch TV all day long. Do a bit of cooking and a lot of eating. I don't see friends for coffee or shopping. Lord help me! My best friend is Oprah! Now that's pretty sad, you must admit.

Yes, of course I felt guilty but I ate another box of cookies and buried the guilt in sweet calories.

Am I ashamed of myself? Absolutely! Am I afraid of the future? Totally! And my biggest fear, the one I have never breathed to a single soul before this minute......" She stopped mid-sentence and gulped air into her lungs to get her through the next part. "............I am *terrified* that Ian has already found a woman more interesting and challenging than his fat, dowdy housewife ruining her life at home."

She turned on her heel and fled from the lounge into the bedroom and threw herself on the bed sobbing into her pillow.

It was easy for everyone to see how hard these words were for Sandra to confess.

She was not alone for long, however. With Zoe hopping along in the rear, all three women crowded around her on the bed, patting her back and offering soothing words of understanding.

It was Valerie, her oldest friend, who dried her tears and made her sit up and listen.

"Remember our motto when we were at college? 'Together against all comers', if I recall it correctly."

Sandra gave a tearful half-smile acknowledging the old saying.

"We are still together and we can fix things. There's still time for that. In case you all think I am Little Miss Perfect, I can tell you my guilt also runs deep and will be with me always."

"What are you saying, Val? What do you feel

guilty about, for goodness sake? Look what you are doing for us here in this special place."

"I don't think you can understand what I am about to tell you unless you have been through a similar situation. You know David died after a long illness but you don't know the price of that illness. Of course David paid the ultimate price but it cost me dearly as well.

When a husband is immersed in a life-or-death struggle like cancer, his wife is left to her own devices in every part of her existence. No one else is there during the sleepless nights and the long, weary days. Who else is there to listen to the fears and worries as successive treatments come and go without alleviating increasingly painful symptoms?

Oh, I can see what you are thinking, Corinne! This is what every wife goes through. You are right. You've seen it many times in the hospital, but does every wife survive by cutting her feelings apart?

By separating herself from the daily trauma and playing a role that only pretends to share the suffering?

I did it to preserve my sanity; to selfishly avoid being drawn down into the abyss, and yet, as months go by, I feel more and more guilty that I betrayed the man I loved. The anger and the resentment grew until I could barely stand it. And all this self-indulgence while he was slowly dying right in front of me."

Corinne was shaking her head in denial of Valerie's claims. Over the years she had seen every version of survivor guilt including close observation of some of the couples who had stayed with her and Arthur during hospital procedures that did not have the same initial happy outcome as David's. She felt she could help Val through this better than the others could and she realized the first step in that healing had already begun, even if Val did not yet know it. First, you have to name it.

Valerie was not finished. She continued in an increasingly quiet voice.

"When we were at Blackwell the other day, I didn't tell you about my special place there. It was the dining room, a calm, beautiful space set for a family meal. I sat there and remembered how, at home, we had to clear out all our dining room furniture, right down to the carpets, so that David's hospital bed and equipment could take its place for his final months. It was his wish to die at home and from that point on there was no denying the inevitable. I was so afraid I would not have the stamina to endure what was to come. I shut up my emotions even tighter and refused every offer of help. I did not dare risk breaking down in public. My control was the only thing I had left. Zoe knows what I am saying."

A nod was all Zoe could summon.

"When it was all over and the remnants of those months were all returned to the hospital, I was unable to enter the dining room; the place where family meals had been enjoyed during the boys' childhoods. It was ruined for me.

I never set foot in it again. It was one of the main reasons I decided to sell the family home and reset my life. When the realtor came to assess the house I asked him to rent furniture for the empty room and I sold the old stuff from the garage where it was stored."

By this point Valerie's voice had almost disappeared and she was clearly exhausted.

"So, Val, you are saying the Blackwell room showed you what you had lost? I am beyond sad for you. You went through this without me and I never did anything to find out what it was like. You said a few minutes ago that our motto still stands. Well, my dearie, that goes both ways. I won't let you be alone again."

It had been a strange time for all of them. There was much to think about and nothing more to be said until there was a chance to absorb the lessons.

Everyone went off to their own beds and silence fell. It was the deep sleep of emptiness. Some pain had been expunged and as yet there was no healing salve to take its place.

That would come later.

Eleven.

Wednesday.

Zoe Morton was astonished to have slept so soundly. After the traumatic confessions of the evening before, she thought she would have tossed and turned all night going over every word that had been said. Instead, she had dreamed of something pleasant and peaceful that left her with no recall of the dream but a calm feeling inside.

She knew, instinctively, a change of venue was required to overcome any lingering emotion of embarrassment among the women. She cast her mind around the options and soon came to a conclusion.

Retail therapy was required.

She consulted with her smartphone while in the bathroom and soon found the perfect place to spend the day. The town of Kendal had a variety of shopping experiences on offer and would fit in with what she wanted to accomplish on her last day with Valerie, Sandra and Corinne.

She tested out her foot by revolving it carefully and was happy with the result. She would be fit for what she intended to be a memorable experience and she was beginning to enjoy flat shoes for a change.

Now to ask Aunt Valerie's approval of her idea.

Valerie was delighted to be relieved of the responsibility of planning this day's events. It was bound to be tricky no matter what she would choose. Added to this dilemma was the rain that had decided to arrive from the cloudy sky, limiting, or cancelling, the options she had thought of. She rapidly agreed to drive the party to Kendal as she knew where the best parking places were in the busy town, rife with one-way streets and pedestrian-only areas.

Together, the two women, conspired to make this day unforgettable, starting with Valerie's quick trip down the lane to Tesco Express for fresh bread and buns, newspapers and some of the lean, tasty bacon that she was unable to get in Canada. British-style bacon rolls would perk up anyone's appetite.

When she returned with colour in her cheeks from this expedition, Sandra had heated the grill and made pots of tea and coffee while Corinne tidied up the apartment and set the table for breakfast.

As soon as the last bun had been consumed and the last of the hot drinks gulped down, the quartet set out for the day's adventures.

The conversation in the car was lighthearted. No one was ready to re-visit the uncomfortable revelations of the previous evening and yet, each heart was lighter of the burdens they had carried alone. Now there would be no way to deny those burdens and, when the time felt right, there would be much more to say about acceptance and healing.

The main road to Kendal wound down past Lake Windermere and the upper part of the town with the same name. It descended rapidly for some twenty minutes more until the last stretch off the highway dropped steeply into the valley where the market town of Kendal lay. Valerie pulled the car into a parking lot beside the bus station and led the group, via an elevator, to the entrance to the Lakeland Centre Shopping Mall.

Sandra was looking for something for her grandchildren. Corinne wanted a special gift for Carla and Valerie stayed with Zoe as she sought advice about what to buy for her personal assistant, Suzanne.

It was decided to reassemble at the High Street mall exit in an hour. Corinne and Valerie laughed to think of the reduced time limit they would have had to adhere to if their husbands were accompanying them.

"I would be lucky to get ten minutes to shop alone!" complained Corinne. "It's so much easier with women!" Corinne and Sandra waved and disappeared into the mid-week crowds.

Zoe and Valerie ended up in a large Boots store where Zoe gave a running commentary on the comparative quality of the cosmetic products on display. It was obvious she thought little of these brands as compared to the Excelsior Range for which she was responsible. Under these circumstances, Valerie wondered what would be a suitable gift for Suzanne. Cosmetics were out of the question and little else was available. After a considerable amount of testing and trying, Zoe chose a new perfume that she estimated would suit her secretary's personality and had the large bottle gift wrapped and placed in a presentation bag.

Valerie had to discourage Zoe from buying items for her. She insisted there was no spare room in her luggage for the return flight to

Canada.

They found a seat near the mall exit and waited there for the others to arrive. Zoe turned from watching the shoppers with their umbrellas hurrying by on the street and warned Valerie that the rest of the day was to be strictly at her expense. Before Valerie could object, she declared it was the least she could do after everything that had happened.

"Surely you don't mean the incident with your foot? That was just what anyone would have done for you."

"No. There's a great deal more I have to thank all three of you for. You accepted me into your close circle and never once complained about my intrusion. You showed me what was missing in my life and you, especially, Aunt Val, if I may call you that?" Valerie nodded, unable to say how much it meant to her to hear the words. "You know how much my mother wanted for me, and you can guess what her loss has done to me even without the circumstances of her death. This intervention of yours has jolted me out of a downward spiral and I have begun to hope for a better future. I promise not to lose touch with you wherever you are when you settle again."

Valerie looked into the dark eyes, so much like

Grace's now that they had lightened a little. She smoothed the wing of dark hair and caressed the girl's cheek as she had seen her mother do when she was just a child. Something lovely and healing passed between them then and the older woman suddenly wished that she could someday create with her daughters-in-law the warmth of affection she now shared with Zoe. The look lingered and ended in a smile. They were enclosed in an invisible bubble, impervious of interruption, devoid of noise and in which, time, itself, had stopped.

Eventually, the passing crowd came back into focus and they saw Sandra and Corinne approaching, laden with bags.

"Right!" announced Zoe. "We're off to Marks and Spencer just across the road here, then lunch and lots more shopping and this time it's strictly for your own consumption and I am paying the bills."

Strenuous objections arose immediately but when Valerie refused to contradict Zoe, the others fell into line behind the pair, arm in arm, and proceeded across the road as instructed.

*

Hours later, replete with food and unable to carry any more of their purchases, the happy shoppers returned to Ambleside in great high spirits. Zoe's plan was not yet completed, however. She had paid attention to, and delivered verdicts on, what was bought by each person with a view to ensuring grand new outfits were obtained. While they were busy trying on garments, she had warned the cashiers who was paying all the bills.

Dresses, Sandra proclaimed totally unsuitable for her lifestyle; shoes and jewellery, Corinne drooled over and a matching leather case and handbag set for Valerie that were outrageously priced, were just some of the treasures they now owned. It was a veritable Christmas in July and each woman was like a delirious child, eager to try on garments and parade for the others' delighted approval.

Zoe let them enjoy the moment and then came the next surprise.

"You may have noticed this box I had delivered the other day. It's full of Excelsior products I selected for you and I want to give each of you a make-over before we all go out to a splendid meal in the new Daffodil Hotel in Grasmere."

Exclamations of sheer delight filled the room. It had been ages since any of them had been treated this extravagantly. In several cases, it was a completely unique experience.

Zoe displayed her products on the dining table and began with the statement; 'Beauty is my Business'.

She then adjusted all the available light sources to focus on the face of the client in front of her.

"As we are going indoors where there will be artificial light, it's important to approximate those conditions to get optimal results with makeup."

She rolled up her sleeves and set to work on Valerie, who, she announced, needed some skin treatments as the North American climate was known to wreak havoc on skin condition. She applied a deep moisturizer then waited while it was absorbed before adding a tinted foundation imbued with a secret ingredient which left a gleam on the skin's surface, virtually concealing any fine lines and wrinkles.

Sandra and Corinne watched with interest. This was a new Zoe. Her expertise was evident. She must have had years of practice with customers before ascending to the upper levels of management.

"Good skin treatment gives a base for everything else you do to enhance the appearance. Now we choose one feature to emphasize. Valerie's best feature is her high cheekbones so I will lightly line her upper eyelids with a brown pencil to complement her hazel eyes, apply mascara of course, and brush her cheeks from centre, toward the top of her ear, with a rose blush containing a little gold pigment for an added glow. A smudge of gold eyeshadow, a brush of gloss on her eyebrows, a pink lip, and she is perfectly prepared for a night on the town...... any town, that is!"

Applause met the conclusion of Zoe's performance and Sandra eagerly took Valerie's seat.

"This will be much more difficult for you, Zoe," she warned. "I rarely use any make-up."

Zoe whispered to her first client that there was something on her bed she needed to see, then turned her attention to Sandra.

"I suspect you have skin breakouts from time to time. Your diet needs more fibre and lots of fruit and vegetables. This will clear up the situation and help you lose excess weight. I will use an excellent concealer cream we have developed at Excelsior. Once this is applied, I can sculpt your face with shadows and highlights so you will look ten pounds lighter."

Sandra's eyes gleamed at the thought. She sat perfectly still.

"Your eyes need definition. I am going to pluck your eyebrows with a patented system guaranteed to be painless. Just tilt your head a little and it will be over in minutes and your face will look transformed."

She smoothed an alcohol swab over the eyebrow area and commenced work with deep concentration.

Corinne could see the change immediately and ran a finger over her own eyebrows wondering if she was eligible for the same process.

"You need a soft grey eyeliner to make your eyes zing," she advised, "but black mascara will do even more for you." Zoe continued to work with a palette of brushes until Sandra's skin was perfected, then sat back and surveyed her work.

"If you don't mind a suggestion, I think you should change your hairstyle. You have lovely thick hair and the grey tones just lighten your natural blonde colour, but the low pony tail doesn't suit you anymore. I'll pull your hair up like this and twist it into a coil. You own hair clip can now anchor your hair in place and this technique acts as a quick facelift."

Sandra rushed off to the bathroom to see the new face and hair and met Valerie coming from the mirror wearing a beautiful dress in shades of her favourite blue.

"Zoe bought this for me," she explained. "And there's a pair of matching shoes. She must have done this while we were in the changing rooms. What can I say?"

"Just say thanks," advised her roommate. "You look wonderful!"

Corinne was now sitting in the client chair awaiting the expert's response. She thought how much this specialized consultation would cost in a store, if she had ever had time or money for such an extravagance. This holiday was turning out to be so much more than she could have hoped for.

"Let me look at you," said Zoe. She turned Corinne's face back and forth to catch the light.

"I have to say I have noticed you flush from time to time and I presume you are experiencing menopause symptoms. Am I right?"

"Yes, unfortunately! I haven't found a medication to help with that yet, so I am often uncomfortable and have to wear a lot of absorbent cotton, especially at night. It plays havoc with my temper, I'm sad to say. I can't wait till this part of my life is over."

"What I can suggest for you is a gel foundation. It has an immediate cooling effect on the skin and can be used several times a day if needed. Fortunately, your skin doesn't require any colour correction other than a little concealer under the eyes when you are not sleeping well."

Zoe applied the gel and Corinne sighed with contentment just knowing she had a solution to this problem on hand.

"Your colouring is quite lovely. Rich brown tones in your hair and eyebrows frame your eyes very nicely. I think your eye colour lies between blue and green but more on the green spectrum when you wear that colour."

"So that's why you got me to choose the emerald satin skirt and top! I adore the sparkle on the boat neckline. Very cunning, Zoe!"

"I must ask, who does your hair?"

"Oh, I just hack at it myself occasionally. Is it too awful?" Corinne raised her hands and ran them through her short locks until the ends stood up all over her head.

"Not at all! It suits you in fact. I would let the ends grow a little more and pull some strands down over your face as a frame. Otherwise your 'chopping' is fine, and inexpensive."

Zoe smiled but then grew more serious, first looking around to ensure the others were busy elsewhere in the apartment. "I notice you are developing a deep wrinkle between your eyes, Corinne. You don't wear glasses so it could be a bad habit of frowning. I might advise Botox...."

"What?"

"..........just in that area. You don't need it anywhere else and it would fix the wrinkle before it gets too deep to be turned around. It would spoil your attractive looks in the long run."

"Well, you've given me good news with the bad, I suppose. Thank you so much Zoe."

"I have samples here for you to keep. There's mascara, of course, and two contrasting eyeshadows you should try plus a big pot of the gel. Your best feature is your lovely full lips. Use only the best lipstick or salves. You'll find some in the box. All of you will have coupons for more purchases from Excelsior and if you can't find them locally, go online for even more discounts."

Zoe bundled Corinne's selection into an Excelsior gift bag and handed it to her.

"Now, *I* must get dressed for this event. I need to compete with the three stunning women I am accompanying!"

Corinne watched Zoe go off to their bedroom and wondered how she could ever have thought the girl cold and distant. Under that polished exterior was a lonely, vulnerable, damaged young woman trying hard to survive yet willing to give so much to others when she had a chance.

It occurred to her to remember this conclusion the next time she was dealing with Carla.

*

The memorable evening at the hotel, lived up to the expectations of each of the women.

Zoe was pleased to see the high level of service for a table presided over by women with no man in sight.

Sandra and Corinne were like a pair of peacocks relishing the glances that came their way from other curious diners, and flourishing their finery at every opportunity.

A dining room manager approached their table and asked if everything was to their satisfaction. Zoe replied in the affirmative and he explained that a hotel resident had asked him who the lovely ladies were and what they might be celebrating. He cast an eye around the quartet in their colourful outfits and accepted the explanation that they were friends on holiday in the area. Bowing to the table he departed with little information and the wish that more of his diners displayed such style and fashion sense. Perhaps he could offer the ladies a voucher for a future visit.

Valerie was beyond delighted at the way the week was working out. She had hoped for changes and more closeness but who could have predicted the role Zoe had played? She smiled to herself every time the girl moved and displayed the red belt and bright fabric rose attached to her elegant black dress. It was proof the changes were coming fast for her also.

Just as Valerie was wondering if she should indulge in another glass of the excellent wine Zoe had ordered, more evidence of her forward thinking appeared.

"I have booked a taxi to take us all home to Ambleside tonight, so drink as much as you want.

Valerie, your car will be safe here overnight and in the morning a taxi will take all of you back to

Grasmere for a day in the village and area. I am sure there are more walks and hills to conquer.

I'll be off early, back to my work life in London but, be assured I will not forget these few days with you. I'll be in touch again soon."

"Let's toast ourselves and the friendships we have made, or re-made, here!" said Valerie, before the tears in her throat threatened to choke off her voice.

Glasses were raised and clinked across the table as the perfect day came to a close.

Twelve.

<u>Thursday</u>

If there had not been a taxi waiting for the women, the day would have been somewhat of a downer after the thrills of Wednesday and the fact that there was now one less in the group.

Corinne had managed a quick word or two before Zoe left for an early departure that would take her to Windermere train station and the connection to London. They exchanged a brief hug and Zoe was gone, leaving a huge gap behind her.

Valerie hustled the others along and ensured they had all the gear required for a day out in Grasmere. She intended to tackle a decent walk at least, this time but, first, there was much to see and do in the village.

Before collecting her car from the parking lot of the hotel, she decided to introduce the women to the tourist attraction which was just across the main road and a short way up a lane.

Dove Cottage, the early home of the Lake District's favourite son, William Wordsworth, had been preserved in its original form so visitors could experience life in the early nineteenth century when the poet had his sister and a young family living with him.

Valerie climbed to the top of the small garden and waited while Sandra and Corinne joined the house tour. The scent of coal fires rose to meet her and like most Scottish-born women of her era, the aroma brought back memories of childhood and the hard work required to feed and heat a family in those far-off times. Gas-powered heating systems had been only one of the great advantages she found when she and David had emigrated to Canada only a few years after they had married.

In the peaceful garden setting, on a wooden bench where Wordsworth had often sat, she thought about those happy, eventful years of her marriage and how the experiences then, had pulled the couple together as they forged a new life in a new land.

Bees buzzed contentedly in the old-fashioned flowering plants that scented the air around her. She wondered if it were possible to dwell more on those happier times and vanquish the sadder memories she now carried with her. Could she do an inventory of her marriage and balance out the bad ending with the greater number of good beginnings? This seemed a suitable place to begin. Wordsworth had sorrows in his lifetime and yet he created poetry that had inspired thousands to think of nature as a healing source and to appreciate the beauties around them.

I can at least make a start, she promised.

Sandra and Corinne emerged from the dark interior of the cottage and exclaimed at the tiny rooms and the number of family and literary visitors who had existed inside the cramped quarters.

"People must have been a lot smaller in those days. I'd have a back spasm just going through the doorways!"

"You could be right," added Sandra. "Did you see the size of the beds?" No one was likely to have sex in one of those. They would fall on the floor if they tried!"

The trio collapsed in laughter at the thought and exited the garden before they were ejected for unseemly levity in a literary shrine.

Once back in the car, they made slow progress

through Grasmere village, avoiding tourists and dogs who stepped into the road without much care for traffic. All three were glad when Valerie pulled in to the public parking beside the gardening centre and they could continue on foot.

"Where to now?" asked Corinne.

Valerie had given this some thought. "I think we have started on a Wordsworth trail today. My feeling is we need some exercise after our extravagant eating lately. What say we begin with an easy walk to warm up and then see where we get to?"

Sandra and Corinne could not deny their guide had a good point. Serious exercise was needed. They had all come equipped and the day was proving to be set for good weather.

"Lead on!" they said in chorus.

Valerie pointed straight ahead from the parking exit and they skirted the outer edge of the village, past the green where visitors waited for buses, and with stops to look in the shop windows they soon reached a lane signposted; Goody Bridge.

"That doesn't sound too challenging!" announced Sandra as she took the lead up the slight slope.

A walk through a small housing estate where they were able to bypass the road on a gravel trail at the side of a farmer's field, took them to the bridge where they paused to look at the rushing waters from the recent rain. Then they diverted left to a track across bumpy fields. The view opened out at this point and they saw they were in a valley with what Valerie called 'fells' on all sides. Since the track proceeded without verging toward a mountain, a term Corinne preferred, they trudged along talking about the quaint houses they had seen and speculating about what it would be like to live in a small community. They saw a few serious climbers, identified by their backpacks and steady, fast paces never varying despite the terrain. These pairs soon got ahead of the trio and by the time they reached a solid road at the opposite side of the valley, they were alone again.

They arrived at a bench by the side of the road and sat there gladly. The reason for the positioning of the bench was immediately apparent as the view was spectacular. Ahead of them rose a mountain almost a perfect triangular shape. From their slight elevation the whole valley could be seen and they could point out places they had passed, looking more interesting from their new perspective.

"You know," began Sandra, "I am realizing we walked here without any sense of the scenery behind us. It's only now we can see the bigger picture and notice what we were missing before."

"That sounds like a deep thought," commented Corinne, when she had swallowed a mouthful of water. "I came to the same conclusion. Is that a message for us, do you think?"

Valerie let the question linger in the air. Her opinion was that Sandra was right on target and Corinne's idea of a message could apply equally in all their situations. It was well worth considering the value of a new perspective in all their lives.

Valerie did not allow a long break as she knew muscles began to cool off quickly and the day's exertions were not over. She led them through a gate marked 'National Trust Property' and the hiking poles came into play as they were on a wooded slope following a rough trail upward. By this time, all three could calculate this increased height was going to provide even better, longer views of the countryside and so it proved. At the top of the hill was a structure of stones where they could sit and look into the next valley previously hidden from them.

"Isn't this magnificent!" breathed Corinne. "I never knew you could see these vistas for such little effort."

"And the air is so clear and cool. In the woods the sun is filtered. I love it. I had forgotten how this felt. It's a feeling I left behind when I left Mull so long ago."

When Valerie led them back to the marked trail they were heading downward again.

"There are two choices here, I think. We'll take the shorter route this time."

To their surprise this choice involved a detour through a low tunnel built of stone. When they emerged from the other side it was to see a square, buff-coloured house below them and a path leading to it through marked garden beds centred around a large well. In moments they were at ground level and approaching the house.

"So, this is where you were taking us, Val? What's here?"

"It's something new to me also. The house is called Allan Bank and was only recently opened to the public. The story is that a Liverpool merchant had the house built in a three year period between 1805 and 1808. William Wordsworth protested about this as the elevated site ruined his view of the woods and hills from Dove Cottage. I think he must have seriously annoyed the original owner as the Wordsworth family moved in that same year, renting it from John Crump."

"I can guess what was said about Crump! Wordsworth had a fine command of language!"

"You're probably right, Sandy. In any case they stayed for only three years after improving the windows to take advantage of the surrounding views. The family moved on to the Rectory in Grasmere."

"Sounds like they were tired of renting and Wordsworth got a job as local vicar. How do you know all this, Val?"

She produced from a pocket a National Trust guide to the property that she had picked up on her recent visit to Grasmere, and flourished it. "Always be prepared!"

"Huh! Always be a teacher, you mean."

"That too! Take a look around and check out the window views. Each and every one is worthy of a painting, they say. The house is a work in progress. Decisions about its final form are still being made. You can make suggestions.

And see if you can find out which kind of tea was preferred by Wordsworth."

"Honestly! Do you teachers ever quit teaching?"

"Never!"

A pleasant hour was spent in and around the house including Valerie's discovery of a medieval chapel nearby that looked ancient until she asked and was told it was used as a billiard and games room by later owners. "Bad decision!" was her response.

Corinne's best find was identifying from a large window, the same terrace above Grasmere Lake that they had all been on a day or so before.

Sandra proudly declared she had located the tearoom in the old kitchen area and learned they served free cups of tea, courtesy of Twinings, a famous London company who sent Wordsworth a chest of their tea every year and were now renewing that tradition for Allan Bank.

"Right! Follow me for lunch," encouraged Valerie.

"Thought you would never ask," groaned Sandra. A quick cup of Twinings' best had not satisfied her hunger but she soon perked up when a short downhill walk from the house took them back close to the spot from which they had started and they were soon in the centre of the village and seated at tables on a balcony overlooking the River Rothay, decorated with a flotilla of mallard ducks bobbing around against the current.

"This was worth waiting for!" declared Sandra, as she settled in her chair and perused the menu.

"It was a favourite spot of David's. He used to drop crumbs from his scone down to the ducks and watch their antics."

"Sounds like a plan to me!" Corinne took charge and ordered afternoon cream teas for all of them, returning from the indoor counter with a heavily laden tray. Sandra had nabbed a table right at the edge of the balcony and there was silence as the women enjoyed the special treat in this lovely location. Visitors passing by on the stone bridge above them looked down in envy at the peaceful scene.

Appetites sated, thoughts turned to other things.

"You and David must have loved it here. No wonder you chose this area for our holiday with you."

Valerie nodded through a last mouthful of cheese scone. "I was worried it might be difficult for me but it has brought back many happy times and that is helping heal the wounds."

"You must realize it is healing wounds for us also, Val, although different wounds of course." Sandra agreed. "I know I have a long way to go. Oprah says we have to forgive ourselves before we can do the work of healing and forgiving others."

Sandra sounded so sincere that her companions did not have the heart to make the usual jokes about her devotion to Saint Oprah. They privately thought she was probably correct. Valerie felt a pang as she thought also of Zoe and the long journey to healing ahead of her.

Corinne changed the subject by stating she had been looking across at the churchyard for the last hour and wondered why so many people were walking around there. "What's so special?"

"Let's go and see!"

The churchyard of St. Oswald's Church was a tree-shaded, peaceful sanctuary where pilgrims came to visit the burial place of the Wordsworth family. Paths snaked through the grassy areas. In spring a host of daffodils would remind visitors of the poet's most famous work. The three friends wandered around and back toward the river where they spied others enjoying the Riverside Restaurant's balcony seats they had only just vacated.

At the same moment, Valerie and Sandra noticed the flagstones on the path beneath their feet were inscribed with names and locations. "Look at this! These are memorial stones. We could do this for Grace and take a picture to send to Zoe. I think she would like that. What do you think?"

"I think it's a brilliant idea!"

"And I know how you can do it!" proclaimed Corinne. She disappeared and returned in a minute brandishing a pamphlet she had spotted in a box at the churchyard entrance.

"You can do this from home. Just fill in the details and they will send the photograph when the stone is laid in place."

Corinne and Sandra backtracked to read more of the inscriptions. Most did not give dates of birth and death only names and sometimes quotes. They concluded the stones commemorated many different events. Valerie followed along with another thought in her mind. This would be the ideal place for her to   place a flagstone for David. Visiting it in its place here would provide an excuse for another trip to the Lake

District. She acknowledged this time and this place had given her the most restorative moments she had enjoyed in many years.

Valerie and Corinne tucked their pamphlets away safely. Sandra looked at her watch and stated the afternoon was not over. Where could they head next?

Encouraged by this enthusiasm, Valerie decided to extend the day with a climbing challenge that would demand all the strength her companions had demonstrated. She led them back to the car park and they drove through the village and out onto the main road. Only a few minutes later, she pulled into a steep lane where cars were lined up along the left side.

"Wait a minute! The sign we just passed said 'Rydal Mount'. Don't tell me that's short for mountain?"

Valerie had just spotted a free parking spot further up the lane and quickly claimed it, as it as just large enough for her car. She carefully backed in before answering Corinne.

"Yes, there is a mountain just ahead of us but you need to know, Wordsworth, whose large, final, family home is off this lane, climbed Rydal Mount for exercise every day of his life."

"Well, now!" proclaimed a confident Sandra,

"It can't be too much of a challenge if he could do it. Let's give it a try!"

Valerie had the idea that the trio would not make it to the heights of the mount but she knew even a shorter ascent would be worth the time and trouble. She and David had attempted this climb and found it to be one of the most satisfying hikes they had ever done. But that was long ago.

Corinne had a spare water bottle, Sandra had the two hiking poles, Valerie had the backpack containing a camera and a small pair of binoculars, and thus prepared they set off up the lane through a farmyard and onto a rocky but well-marked track that led straight upward.

At first, their attention was on their footing. Rocks of various sizes had been pushed to the side when the path was made and all three were conscious of the need to place their booted feet carefully. The track twisted around a vertical hillside and they were soon puffing for breath as each step was on a steep incline. This was no easy access like the White Moss climb of two days ago.

"I need to stop to catch my breath," begged Sandra.

"Good thought," agreed Valerie, and they

disposed themselves on the next large rock that presented itself. As soon as their breathing had returned to normal, it was obvious that their efforts had been rewarded. The lane below had disappeared and the view encompassed both the lake and the hills on the opposite side of the main road. The lake was still, tranquil, and reflected both the surrounding blue sky and the green hills. As they watched in awe, white clouds sailed across the sky and their shadows traversed the entire landscape. It was something they would never have seen at ground level.

Valerie told them it was called Rydal Water. "I think Wordsworth must have thought the climb worth the effort to see this." She took several photographs.

"And, we're nowhere near the summit yet!" added Corinne. "What about it, ladies, are you game for more?"

They passed around the water bottle and vowed to keep going for a few minutes more. Valerie recognised her friends were succumbing to 'climbers' fever' the desire to see if the next panorama would be better than the previous one. She promised herself not to allow the beginners to push beyond their strength. Corinne was younger, but Sandra and Valerie were going to suffer for it if they overused these new muscles.

One more turn of the track brought them to a wide, expansive view in another direction. Fields of sheep bordered the main road far below and in the distance a lush green valley followed a river filled with rushing water from the previous day's rain. They looked in silence broken eventually by Corinne's quiet voice. "I have just realized we will have to go back down this mountain again. I think it's time to retreat."

"I agree," breathed Sandra. "But it has been so worth the effort. How Wordsworth managed this in his later years is beyond my understanding but I can see why he would want to try. It must have been quite a sight in all seasons."

They gathered up their belongings and their remaining strength and carefully made their way down the mountainside with Valerie in the lead to prevent any slips or falls. Descending uses a different set of muscles and she was keen to keep the day's delights as a good memory, unmarred by accident.

By the time they reached the car, all three were ready to admit defeat.

"I can't wait to slip into that hot tub," sighed

Sandra.

"Exactly what I was thinking," admitted Corinne.

Valerie agreed, and drove them back to Ambleside in the silence of deep contentment.

There was still an evening ahead of them to relax, recover and, she hoped, revisit some of her original intentions for this reunion.

*

All three donned pyjamas and settled down before the patio windows with glass in hand to enjoy the evening sunlight on the hills. They had dined well on microwaved meat pies and baked beans with bakery bread and a cream trifle from the fridge.

Feet raised on footstools, they reviewed the day and laughed together like old friends. As darkness fell, Sandra turned on the television for the first time since she arrived, commenting on how it was her daily companion at home and how she had truly not missed it with all the excitements of the week.

They watched a comedy series which Sandra recommended but when it was over she confessed it had lost its charm for her. "I don't know how to explain it, but something has changed in me. It's like the feeling on the mountain when you see a new perspective you never had imagined possible."

Corinne instantly echoed her sentiments. "For me, the mountain views had two aspects. There was the godlike sense of being far above and watching the tiny cars and tinier people going about their business without knowing they were being observed, and the opposite sense of how very small we humans are set against the sheer magnificence of nature in the raw."

"This conversation has taken a decidedly philosophical turn," remarked Valerie.

"Well, it just proves how trivial that TV program was." Corinne turned to Sandra. "Look, I'm not trying to disparage you. Anything that gets you through the day is all right by me. If I had had a chance to distract myself by watching TV I might have been more easily satisfied with my working days and nights. There never seemed to be the time to do it."

Sandra shrugged. "It's true that what we have been through together this week makes the average half-hour comedy look totally inconsequential. I am reminded of a book I saw in a Kendal bookshop.

I was looking around for books to take home for my grandchildren and they had this book on display.

It was titled; 'Letters to My Former Self' and it made me think what advice I should be giving to my grandchildren to save them from my mistakes."

"Did you buy the book? It sounds like something I could use for Carla."

"No. And now I wish I had."

Valerie put down her glass and heaved a deep sigh. "Ladies, you may not believe this, but before I came here I made a list of questions to ask each of you. It was similar to the book Sandy described. I was hoping we could get into real discussions using the questions but, of course, I could never have imagined the things we have already revealed to each other."

Sandra looked at Corinne and saw reflected in her face the same curiosity she was feeling.

"Val, go and get your list. It sounds more interesting than anything on TV."

Corinne refilled their wine glasses. Sandra pulled her chair closer to the leather couch and arranged the cushions. She suspected this was going to be a long session.

The list of questions was in Valerie's hand when she returned from the bedroom. She went to place it on the coffee table for all to see, when Corinne snatched it up and returned it to her.

"You choose the questions you think have the most relevance for us now. We don't need to see them first. We just have to pledge to be truthful about our answers."

She cast a glance at the other two and received a nod to confirm their commitment.

Valerie cleared her throat and took a quick sip from her glass. Suddenly, what had once seemed like a fairly innocuous parlour game activity, assumed an importance far beyond her original intent. She now knew enough about her companions' lives to predict the impact of their answers. She also understood this session could not have been viable before they had reached this level of intimacy with each other.

"If you insist, I'll start with the question that most closely resembles Sandra's book.
If you could talk to your teenage self, what advice would you offer her?"

Her two listeners sat back in their seats. This was not going to be an easy question to answer.

The silence lasted for two long minutes until Valerie decided to take the bull by the horns.

"I've probably had more time to consider this one, so I'll begin.

I would tell her that life is long, don't rush into anything.

Choose your friends wisely. With luck, they will be with you always.

Protect your heart. It is easily damaged."

Neither of her listeners said anything. Both were too busy considering how her words fit with their own life experiences.

Finally, Corinne smiled at Valerie and took over.

"I would give that girl a shake and tell her to be much more adventurous. To look for opportunities to enlarge her life, see new places and meet new people.

I'd tell her she is different looking but much more attractive than she thinks she is.

I'd warn her not to marry too soon. It takes time to learn that love is more than sex."

She stopped; then added. "The problem with that girl is she never did listen to good advice."

Valerie and Sandra laughed with Corinne, but Sandra soon became solemn as she realized it was her turn next and there was no way to get out of responding.

"This is hard for me. I think I have been blotting out my true feelings for years with distractions like TV. I'll try to be honest now. It's time.

First of all, I would say to that girl; Wake up! Listen to your own heart. Don't just follow along with others who tell you what you should do.

Second of all (and this is thanks to you, Val) I would tell her to look around her. The island where she was born is magical and special and she will never be truly at home anywhere else."

Her listeners moved closer as they saw tears drop from Sandra's eyes. They understood how important these statements were.

"Thirdly, I would say don't marry at all if it means you could lose yourself. That loss is worse than anything else you can imagine."

No one knew what to say. This one question had opened up a real can of worms. The words echoed in the room and inside each head.

Valerie wondered if it was obvious to the others that her words to her teenage self were also relevant to her present situation.

Corinne suddenly saw that her advice was for Carla as much as for her earlier self.

Sandra knew she had revealed more about her marriage and her fears than she had intended.

Corinne figured they had gone too far to turn back now.

"Well, let's see what the next question brings up. Are we willing to continue?"

It was the same question asked on the Rydal Mount climb. Going on had been the right response then, leading to new understandings. Perhaps it would be the same now.

No one objected, so Valerie looked again at her list. She almost skipped the next question but decided the effects so far demanded its serious consideration. In any case, Corinne was likely to inspect the list and accuse her of a lack of courage if she failed to keep to the plan.

Did you choose the right man to marry?

It was like a bomb dropped into the room and left everyone gasping for air. This was a question every woman thought about in secret and was afraid to answer. Now they were being asked to answer in public.

"I'll tackle this one, if you like." Corinne sat up straight. A deep frown appeared between her eyes as she admitted she had thought long and hard about this when Carla's marriage fell apart. "I think it's a combination of factors leading to whoever you choose. The field may be narrow, especially if you decide to marry early. Your experience with the opposite sex is limited at best, so it's a lottery."

"And don't discount the overwhelming power of sexual attraction," burst out Sandra. "All of those things make the choice very dangerous. Didn't our mothers warn us about it?"

Valerie jumped in with a different point of view. "What about all the numinous elements?"

"The what?"

"What does that mean?"

"I'm talking about the things that are immeasurable, like the idea that opposites attract and the possibility that something within us knows what we will need before we do and, of course, the theory that it doesn't matter who we choose anyway."

"Valerie Westwood! What's got into you? Explain yourself."

"Well, I think it depends on whether you believe there is one perfect man for you. Do you?"

Neither woman listening could ascribe to that theory. Defining the perfect partner would in itself be difficult and would require a kind of self-knowledge seldom available to the young women each of them had been when their marriage decisions were made.

Corinne said she thought the supposed perfect man would vary according to the stage of marriage the woman had reached. "The husband I needed when the babies were small was not the one I would have chosen at the beginning."

"So, are you saying a woman needs several different men throughout her life? And do you think that applies to men as well?"

"Sandra, you've really opened a can of worms there. I'll bet this very subject is often mulled over in many a boozy male drinking establishment across the nation."

When the giggles stopped, Valerie returned to her question. "If it isn't the perfect man, then does it matter which man you marry?"

"Yes."

"No."

"Maybe."

"Look here, Val's probably right. Whoever the man is and whoever the woman, marriage is a series of compromises. Sometimes it's smooth sailing and other times it's stormy seas. If a couple can't deal with that they won't last long."

"Is that what happened with Carla?"

"I can't answer you. I don't know. She hasn't been able to tell me with all the shouting I have been subjecting her to." She glanced away as the truth of this impromptu response sunk in.

Sandra had a puzzled look on her face. "But what happens when the couple drift apart; *so far apart* they lose each other altogether?"

"Then it's about communication, I guess," offered Valerie. "The marriage experts say communication is the number one skill you need to have, but that is so easy to say and damn near impossible to achieve when the red flags are flying."

"Corinne, do you believe the old adage 'never go to bed angry'?"

"Ha! It sounds good, all right, but how many serious quarrels can be settled by bedtime? I call that papering over the cracks and the cracks would open up again pretty soon. It wouldn't work with me and Arthur. With our schedules we are rarely in bed at the same time these days."

Corinne took a breath. She was getting hot in body and mind with this exchange between her and Sandra. She turned to Valerie to take the focus off herself.

"You are asking the questions, Valerie, but not answering so much. What do you really think about this compatibility issue?"

Valerie walked to the patio window where the view had darkened with the setting sun. Her answer was somewhat muffled, but clear enough to be heard by her listeners.

"I agree with most of what you two have said. Marriage, whether long or short, is just as difficult today as it was back in our day. I don't envy young people with all the demands of career and family combined with their greater expectations for immediate personal happiness.

I am thinking about what Zoe told us. Her parents' marriage had gone very wrong somewhere and the results were catastrophic. We can't know, and neither did she, whether it was a lack of communication or a lack of compromise or a failure to meet each other's needs in the bedroom. It's a true saying that no one knows what goes on in another's relationship.

My own marriage must have looked good from the outside. Certainly it lasted a very long time. Was it always happy? No. The years when we were parents with very demanding careers and we had the two boys at home, were busy and difficult. Our holidays here in the Lakes were the only times we could really connect again in a meaningful way. It leaves a lot of months of lonely struggle in between.

David's illness brought us together again in a

deeper way. He needed me as he had not needed me for years. It was a testing time for both of us. If I had to say what kept me by his side through the worst of it, I think it was a matter of loyalty. I could not have abandoned him to strangers. If nothing else, we had such a long shared history together and that creates a shorthand in communication. Who else could have known that when David's left ear twitched he was hiding something?

When all else falls away there is no one else in the whole world who knows you that well."

She remained by the window, her breath fogging on the glass. The hills directly ahead gradually lost all features. Trees, fields, houses, paths, rocks, succumbed to the darkness until there was only a black shape against the fading indigo of the evening sky. It was symbolic of the way her life with David had slowly come to its end. She was conscious that, in a few hours from now, God willing, the sun would bring colour back to this scene. She felt hope for a similar renewal in her life. Without a doubt this week had been a watershed.

Answers? It was too early for those, but there was such comfort in the companionship of these friends.

Behind her in the silence of the darkened room, Sandra felt again the anguish of knowing she had been oblivious to the suffering of her old friend. She had wasted months with trivial time-wasting activities when she could have been a support, even if at a distance.

It was too late now. Shame filled her, not just for her neglect of Val, but also for the neglect she had imposed on her whole life.

David had gone too soon. Who knew how much time was left to any one of them?

She reached down into parts of herself long ignored. She was determined to take charge of her life again before it was too late.

Corinne suddenly remembered tomorrow was her last day in this beautiful place. She was not sure what would happen when she returned home but she was sure it would be something different. This brief time apart from her ordinary existence had jolted her into a new world where things she had accepted as permanent, if not exactly productive of happiness, were seen in a fresh way. There was a lot of thinking to be done yet but she felt as if she must seize any opportunity to make things better for her family. This week had opened doors in her mind. Doors she was unwilling to close.

It was all thanks to Valerie Westwood, the woman whose back she was now studying.

Corinne picked up the paper Valerie had left on the coffee table. She scanned the remaining questions and saw several had already been dealt with in their discussion, but there was one question she felt would bring the evening, and the week, to a close with a more positive vibe.

"Valerie, I am about to make a large pot of tea. Before we conclude this evening's session can I ask if we all answer one last question from your list?

Valerie turned and resumed her seat. "Of course we can. What's the question?"

What is your greatest desire?

"That's easy. I want to do better, and be better." Sandra smiled at each of them.

"I need to start over," said Valerie with a nod to each friend.

"I desire to never forget the lessons I have learned here and to value forever the events of this amazing week. All three exchanged a high-five at Corinne's words.

"Now let's relax and drink tea!"

Thirteen.

<u>Friday.</u>

Sandra wakened as soon as the morning light stole between the long curtains of their bedroom window.
She glanced over at the twin bed where Valerie was still sleeping peacefully. The last thing she recalled from the night before was a quiet conversation they had shared in the dark. Valerie had told her the agenda for their final day and Sandra had been pleased to hear it was to be a local exploration.
She felt full of energy and thought a swim in the pool would be a fine start to the day and significant of the changes she had decided to make.
She knew where the pool key was so she slipped into her swimsuit in the bathroom, pulled slacks and a jumper over the top and stuffed underwear into the pockets. Towels were

supplied at the pool. With any luck she would be back and ready for the day before the others awoke.

Valerie heard the sound of the apartment door closing. She stretched and saw Sandra's bed was empty.
She did not make a move to get up. It was good to have a minute to gather her thoughts. So much had happened in a few short days. She mentally reviewed her aims and objectives for the holiday and found most had already been met or exceeded. There were many places the group had not seen and those castles, towns and climbs would have to wait for another occasion. She felt sure there would be another opportunity; if not in the Lake District, somewhere else.
Her thoughts turned to Zoe and not for the first time. How was she getting on back in London in her own, familiar environment? Would she continue contact with them or put the incidents of this week behind her? It seemed likely she would find it easier to wipe it all from her mind, particularly the painful parts, but it was those parts that had released some of her anguish about Grace. More than once, Valerie had seen a

shadow of Grace in Zoe's face despite her greater resemblance to her father. In a way it was as if Grace had been looking down on them this week. She hoped so.

She yawned widely and shifted mental gears. There were things to be done today. She must settle up with the office, pack her new bags, do some tidying and make use of the rest of this day. It should be memorable as well as a fitting conclusion to the week. Tomorrow she would set off early for the airport and the flight home to Canada.

Corinne was padding around the bedroom looking at the clothes she had pulled out of the closets and spread over the spare bed. She was wondering if Valerie would donate her old suitcase to her so she could pack these new clothes. The hiking boots took up a lot of space as well as the gifts she had bought for Carla and Arthur. There was no way she would risk crushing the gorgeous satin skirt and top Zoe had chosen for her. It was laid over the pillows on the spare bed and she could not help admiring its beautiful green tones.

The thought occurred to her that she might never wear such an item again. Where would she go in such an outfit? She dismissed the thought immediately. Negative thinking was to be banned from her future life. She would find, or create, a suitable event if necessary. Gone were the days when practical, washable work clothes were all she ever wore. This dress was the good omen she needed to remind her there was more to life than work and worry.

She had been awake for hours, sitting on the bed and watching the dawn light transform the hills. She had never closed these drapes after Zoe left. It was such a treat to move around a bedroom knowing she was free from the prying eyes of neighbours. She had fallen asleep with moonlight and starshine instead. As far as she was concerned, anyone who was out on those hills with binoculars was very welcome to all they might see of her through the windows. It was freeing to have the time to relish the beginning of a day without the pressures of having to do so much in a short time before work or the need to close out the day and get much-needed sleep after nightshift. She had often thought it was a vampire existence not suited for human beings.

The sun was well up now. She had moved around quietly hoping not to disturb her companions.

She decided to squeeze every last ounce of joy out of this final day. There would be no sad farewells from Corinne Carstairs.

*

Valerie returned from the office with a letter in her hand. "Look at this you two! It's an actual hand-written letter from Zoe. Can you believe it in these days of text and e mails?"

Corinne and Sandra looked up from their coffee cups and waved Valerie out to the balcony where they were discussing the ever-entertaining view.

"So what does it say, Val? It must be important to make a busy business woman take time to put pen to paper. And I see it's a Courier delivery. *Very important* then!"

She carefully removed the single sheet of letter-headed paper from the envelope and proceeded to read it aloud. There could be nothing in it that would be a surprise to any of them after all they had heard this week.

Dear Aunt Valerie ,
I did not want Suzanne to write this for me.

It's too personal.

You will be interested to know she has said repeatedly that my holiday has done me a lot of good and it was long overdue. I can't argue with any of that but she has no idea yet exactly how much good it has done.

There is no possible way to thank you enough. I extend this to both Sandra and Corinne, of course. It was a combined effort of kindness and concern that has enabled me to come this far so soon.

I will start by saying I have found a good therapist and he is keeping me centred.

I am seeing my life through new eyes now and the changes are coming fast.

Blackwell showed me how cold and impersonal my loft apartment is. I am looking for a move to somewhere with a view and a warmer vibe.

My makeover session with you reminded me how much I enjoyed the personal contact with customers. I plan to revitalise that department and coach my staff on the importance of catering to a more mature client.

Suzanne supports my shorter work day and she is guarding my agenda like a hawk.

I have done some online clothes shopping and there are a few more colours appearing.

Best of all, I now have a purple streak in my

hair, although it is only evident when I wear my hair pinned back with a clasp. Evening occasions only.

There's a long way to go, of course, but I hope you will approve of the first steps.

Please keep in touch and keep me honest.

Forever yours,

Zoe Morton.

"Oh my God! It's a love letter, Val!"

All three were wiping tears from their eyes. They exclaimed at the detail, the speed and the transformations they were hearing about. They had to ask themselves how long it had been since Zoe left.

"It's no wonder she's such a success in business. She's a whirlwind when she gets going."

Valerie looked at Sandra. "We have to support her, Sandy. She's right about the hard road ahead. I will have to depend on you since I am so far away but I will do everything I can so she knows she will never be alone again.

"I know I am not as close to Zoe as you two are but I am still willing to step in when needed and I am nearer to London than either of you."

"Of course you are, Corinne! I didn't mean to

exclude you from this. Any help you can give will be much appreciated. Your medical knowledge could be helpful. She has a lot of trauma to deal with."

Corinne looked down for a moment. She wanted to keep her eyes concealed in case they revealed something she had not confessed to the others, or to anyone. For a short period, several years ago, she had been unfaithful to Arthur with a young student doctor at the hospital. Because of this she had a connection to Zoe that could be crucial when the subject of her father's adultery had to be dealt with in therapy.

"We'll all pull together," continued Valerie. Perhaps our next holiday could be in London? Meanwhile cards, texts, e mail, phone calls, or whatever you like, will keep us up to date. I do not want to lose touch ever again with any of you."

"Not going to happen, Val.
 Now, what about today's plans? What should we prepare for this time?"

*

An hour or so later, after a walk around Ambleside's lanes finding unexpected treasures, they stopped for a break in Esquires Coffee Shop enjoying the variety of drinks, snacks and equally interesting actions on the streets outside the corner windows.

"I didn't expect a bowling green here," said Sandra, between mouthfuls of chocolate muffin. "There are so many restaurants and facilities it's no wonder this is a mecca for visitors."

"I loved seeing the inside of that church whose spire is so prominent from our balcony when we look down at the town. It was lovely to hear the bells the other evening when the ringers were practising for Sunday services. I guess we will be far away when those bells ring again."

"Now don't let's get maudlin, ladies. We still have hours to enjoy before we head for the station.

Fasten up your climbing boots. We are off to get an overview of the town you have just been seeing at ground level."

"Another climb?" groaned Corinne.

"You will like this one. It's much easier than Rydal and very close by."

A short walk from the café led straight to a huge park hidden from the main road and accessed from a lane between the church of St. Mary's on one side, and a primary school on the other. At once the outlook changed from the three storey buildings of the town to the distant, expansive views of the surrounding mountains. The trio stood still to take it all in.

"This parkland is so flat. There must be a river here somewhere."

"You're right, Sandy. We are heading there now after a pleasant walk across flat ground. Watch out for the giant old rocks in the middle where the trees are, and the standing stones the children from the school have made."

The path arrived at a quaint humped stone bridge over the river, as promised, and a sharp turn right, over a cattle grid followed by a left onto a wide paved road, soon got their leg muscles warming up.

"Where does this road go?" puffed out Corinne. "I can't see beyond the next bend. It looks like we are aiming for woods but a wide road like this is not just for climbers."

"I think it's an access road for whoever lives up here on the hillside above the park. The fields belong to local farmers. I wonder if we will recognize their homes. We've certainly spent hours memorizing the view from our balcony."

Valerie did not comment. She was looking ahead for the slate steps set into a boundary wall giving right of entry to the upper reaches of Tod Crag. It was years since she had been up here and she did not want to miss the marked track. People could get lost in these linked mountain ranges. She did not intend to be one of those people especially not on this last day of the week.

The road continued to rise steeply, curving again past a house with fine views on three sides and, at last, Valerie spied the steps she had been looking for.

"All right troops! Carefully up here and we will be in the woods for a short distance. Fear not! We have already climbed up half the way to the top."

"Thank God for that!" murmured Corinne.

Sandra could not wait to get back into the open. She knew by now the scenery would be amazing at this height. "I'll lead on for a bit, Val."

The others let her go ahead. If Valerie remembered correctly, there was a short wooden bridge ahead and a sheep gate at its end. They would catch up with Sandy there.

"Be careful, Alexandra! I have to deliver you back to your family today."

"So that's how she got the name Sandy! It's short for Sandra *and* Alexandra."

"She's named after both her father and her grandfather, Alexander Halder. Alexandra was always her 'Sunday' name, or the one the family used when she was in trouble. When we were in college together, she was called by her full name as that was the way she was registered. It was weeks before she told me she preferred Sandy."

"Well, I must say, Sandy has really taken to this climbing lark. She loves it."

"It seems to remind her of her early years in Mull, I think. That's not a bad thing. We all need to respect our beginnings as we get older and wiser."

"How did *you* get to be so wise, Valerie? I don't remember you being so confident when we first met so many years ago?"

"Ah, I was a different person then, Corinne. I was worried about my husband and so many other things. Coming back to the UK under those circumstances, leaving children behind, was a bad time for me. I don't think I am really wise. I have made plenty of mistakes along the way but I hope I have grown from them."

"You've made no mistake with this week, Valerie Westwood. I am so grateful for all you have done for me. I feel renewed and more myself than I have been in years. I have loved being outdoors so much."

They soon found the bridge and squeezed past the sheep gate onto the foot of a hillside stretching upward.

They were now out of the shady wood and into bright sunshine.

"This is going to be hot work!" proclaimed Corinne. "But I am ready for it!"

"Me too!" echoed Sandra from her perch on a rock a few yards ahead. "Is this the right track? I didn't want to get too far ahead."

"Yes, go on. As long as you keep to the well-marked tracks you will get there safely all right. Don't wander off, even if it looks OK."

Valerie watched the two scramble up, like a couple of schoolgirls, competing for the pole position with laughter ringing out around them. She took a deep breath and closed her eyes for a moment.

Seven days.

A short time in anyone's life, but so much had been achieved in this week. In many ways, it had turned out to be much more than she had dared to hope for. Of course, a lot was due to the magic of this glorious part of England. Like Wordsworth wrote, you would have to be dead not to be moved by this grandeur.

She was suddenly overcome with longing for those who were not here to benefit. David and Grace were gone and yet their memories, their essence, had surrounded and encouraged her since she had arrived.

She felt as if Zoe's letter was proof of their intervention. In some ways she felt guided by them. Certainly, she had to admit she was pleased with the results. If the others felt as imbued with optimism as she now felt, things would be improved in all their lives. She could only hope so.

She hitched her backpack higher on her shoulders and set off up the track to the heights from where they would see the town of Ambleside in miniature on its own mountain and valley far below them and, ahead, to their right, the length of Lake Windermere gleaming in the summer sunlight.

*

The day's delights were not over for Valerie Westwood. As the three women were relaxing after an alfresco lunch beside the Rothay River in Ambleside, Valerie got a phone message to tell her to return to the apartment as she had a visitor waiting. There was no clue as to the identity of the visitor. The message had come from the Lakelands' office staff.

"Who do you think it could be?"

"I can't imagine, but I'd better go and find out."

"Just as well you didn't get the call when we were on top of Tod Crag," laughed Corinne.

"I would have ignored it, for sure. It was so beautiful up there and a fitting end to our holiday."

Sandra stirred herself from a half-doze resulting from salad, sandwiches and cake consumed with relish and much appreciated after her physical effort on the mountainside. "Val, why don't you go ahead?

I'm not fit to climb that steep lane yet and I really want to look into the shop with the crystals and rocks for something for my grandkids."

"I'll stay with Sandra. We'll join you in a while and don't worry. I've got my eye on the clock."

Valerie set off along the main street and past the bank building to the lane. As she climbed steadily upward for what she realised would be the last time, she looked around her at the quaint houses descending to her right, crowded together on the hillside so she could look into their tiny front door areas and spy through their kitchen windows. Their gardens were on the left of the lane and ascending upward, but still planted with flowering bushes and tall trees at the summit of the view. Not an inch of the precious space was wasted. It was a philosophy she had grown to admire.

These cottages perched on a hillside, couldn't be more different from her surroundings in Kilworth. She realized she had not given one single thought to her housing dilemma since arriving here. There had been no time with everything happening so fast. A sigh escaped her when she reached the final two steps to the Lakelands' street and paused to catch her breath.

Tomorrow she would be back in Canada and all of this around her would dissolve into a dream and she would be alone again.

But first, the mysterious visitor!

She headed for the office and was amazed to find a familiar figure there.

"It's Jean, isn't it? Jeanette's mother? What a surprise to see you again. What can I do for you?"

"Valerie, I'm so glad you remember me. I was

half afraid you would be gone back to Canada by now but Jeanette checked for me and you won't believe what has happened. George and the children are here and all of us will be in your apartment for the next week."

"That's amazing! But let's go there now and you can tell me how all this came about."

They went down the steps together and walked out to the balcony entrance. Jean was astounded at the view and asked if they could stay outside to enjoy the vista. Valerie agreed and waited till Jean was settled comfortably on a chair before she began her explanation.

"Well, Jeanette and I had such a grand time in Grasmere and we talked about it so much that George decided we should all return for a family holiday. Anna Drake's apartment was not booked for this next week so she suggested we should take it over when your party vacates it tomorrow.

For the last day or so we've been staying in the annex of The Gold Rill Hotel where we met, and George has a whole plan of visits for the children. Liam is a Beatrix Potter fan and Annette is just getting into the books although she thinks Miss Potter has something to do with the famous Harry."

The two women laughed, and Valerie took the chance to ask where Jean's family were at the moment.

"They are all at a Beatrix Potter Exhibit off the Ambleside market square. They will come and collect me in an hour so we don't have much time."

This sounded urgent to Valerie. She asked no more questions and let Jean reveal what was obviously weighing on her mind.

"You see, Valerie, after our brief time together in the hotel, I realized we had a great deal in common.

We are both recent widows who live in Canada and have ties to the UK. I got the sense that your family in Vancouver were not exactly welcoming. Forgive me if I am treading on private matters, but I want to offer you a compromise that might help the situation."

Valerie's attention was now totally focussed on the speaker. She had already been astonished at what had developed from a very brief encounter a week before and now she was hearing about an offer of help. She could not guess what might come next.

"When I leave England, I will be alone in my home in English Bay. It's a beautiful part of the city and I have lived there since Jeanette was born. I won't be moving to Scotland, despite all Jeanette can say. They have their own lives. I need to be where I am most comfortable and I hope to have them all stay with me sometimes, now that the children are older."

She stopped for a breath and smiled at her companion.

"Don't worry! I'm getting to the part that concerns you. You see, Valerie, I have plenty of room for you if you come to see your son and his family. I know, from friends who travel to see their relatives, that living in crowded conditions in homes where there are children and busy lives on the go all the time, can be wearisome to say the least. Jeanette and George have been marvellous but I know it's a strain coping with an older person's diet and sleep requirements. I can see already the accommodations in this apartment will give me some privacy. Anna Drake said it sleeps six comfortably."

Valerie nodded to confirm Jean's last statement but her head was swimming with so much information.

"Let me see if I am following you, Jean. Do you mean," she began hesitantly, "you want me to stay with you in Vancouver?"

"That's right! I guess I've gone the long way around the main point but I feel we can be friends and having a place to stay could help the situation with your daughter-in-law. My travelling friends have told me that is the trickiest relationship and so many families in Canada are separated by the distances between where they used to live and where they now work. It is difficult to remain close when you are so far apart from loved ones most of the time."

Valerie was beginning to understand where Jeanette got her voluble style. The two women were alike in many ways, their generosity of spirit being one of them. She knew she had to respond before an uncomfortable silence developed.

"I am truly overwhelmed by your offer, Jean. I can't believe you have spent time thinking about my issues and come up with such a wonderful solution. Of course, I am delighted to accept your kindness.

I have to agree that having a place to retreat to would make things easier when I visit Vancouver. We'll exchange information so we can keep in touch when you return home, and thank you so much. I am so pleased we met that night."

Jean was rummaging in a capacious handbag for her notebook and pen but she looked up to remark how unexpected meetings can be life changing.

Valerie thought about how Sandra and Corinne had first come into her life and here was another encounter that looked as if it would be equally beneficial.

Just then, the doorbell rang. Valerie went to the door and found her companions, laden with more shopping, and eager to get their final packing done. She quickly filled them in about her visitor and all four had a few minutes to meet and talk before Jean's family arrived to collect her.

Valerie invited the McLennans inside to inspect their accommodations, the extent of which seemed to please them greatly.

Liam and Annette headed immediately to the balcony and exclaimed at the birds flying past so close to them. Liam spotted a small black cat roaming along the path below and was all for going down to pet it. His mother dissuaded him with a promise to do that very thing if the cat appeared again.

George tried the Murphy-style bed that folded down from a large closet in the lounge while Jeanette looked to confirm there was a bath in one of the bathrooms for the children to bathe in.

The family then exited quickly after handshakes all round. The considered opinion of the three women was that the McLennans were an exceptionally nice family and when Valerie shared her conversation with Jeanette's mother, they were vocal about her good luck in meeting the ladies at the hotel.

Sandra and Corinne were keen to ask more questions but Valerie pointed to her watch and urged them to complete their packing. They had trains to catch.

*

The hired car was full of luggage, parcels and bags. Corinne had Valerie's old case as well as the one she had arrived with and Sandra seemed to have bought out a shop or two judging from the extra items she had jammed into carrier bags. Valerie realized the women were fortunate not to have to abide by the restrictions now in place on air travel. Her two new leather cases from Zoe were almost packed and nothing else could be added. She had exchanged photographs with Sandra before they left the apartment. Both of them had forgotten their intentions to share them together but exchanging seemed to be a good substitute. They would phone or e mail each other with comments and questions.

Corinne was delivered to Windermere Station for her train south in good time. It was a tearful goodbye although her farewells had already been said.

Sandra and Valerie waited until the train pulled away, then jumped back into the car for the downhill drive to Kendal and the Oxenholme Station.

"What a fine day we had with Zoe in Kendal," said Sandra as Valerie negotiated the fast winding race track that was the main road to the town at the lowest point of the Lake District. "I can't remember such an all-round good time as that day. Food, friends and beautiful gifts, it was truly memorable and the meal in The Daffodil Hotel was the perfect ending, don't you think?"

"I do agree with you, Sandy, but the best part of all for me was seeing Zoe emerge from her hard shell and become the daughter Grace had always wanted her to be. That is a true transformation and we were all privileged to be there at the start of it. She will be an amazing woman when she gets to grips with the problems that have been holding her back from happiness."

There were a few moments of silent contemplation in the speeding car until Valerie asked, "What about you, Sandy? What has the week meant to you?"

"I am not sure I am able to explain it properly, yet, Val, but you have known me long enough to be aware that I had moved far away from the girl I used to be. I was confident as a mother with my girls clustered around my knees but when that part of my life was over, I seemed to lose my way, or maybe I lost my husband. I don't know. I have a lot of thinking to do and fences to mend but without the kick start of this week with you, I am afraid the impetus to examine my life would never have happened and I dread to think what I was becoming. All I can say for sure is, I am determined not to sink back into the creature I was. Grace's death has taught me life is too short for wasting one moment of it. Zoe taught me changes are possible."

Valerie was glad her attention was on the road ahead and she had to concentrate on her driving. If the two old friends had been face to face, Sandy might not have had the courage to open up as she had just done. It was an important step for her.

"Don't think you are alone in your feelings, Sandy. I have had very similar thoughts about my own life. David's death concentrated my mind remarkably. I don't know how many years I have left but the next list I make will be one that emphasizes the possibilities of my future. It won't be a future without you in it, Sandy. You can be sure about that, my dear."

Sandra put her hand gently on the one nearest to her on the steering wheel and squeezed for a second.

"That's a deal! No more years of separation, I promise."

"I promise too."

The train north to Scotland was an express. A rush of air heralded its arrival and no sooner was Sandra seated than it departed again, leaving Valerie standing alone on the platform as the arriving passengers divided to pass her like a stream flowing past a large rock.

She did not want to move. She wanted to clasp

to her every word and every sensation of the last week before they vanished like the train speeding on to another destination.

Eventually, she had to walk away. She had to drop off the hired car in the Kendal office and take a leisurely bus ride back to Ambleside with a chance the driver rarely gets, to enjoy the scenery one last time. There was a quiet evening awaiting her with little left to do. She thought she would write a few notes for Jean and the McLennans and leave these at the office.

Her cases were packed.

She would rise very early to take a taxi to Windermere and catch the train to Manchester Airport and her plane ride to Toronto. Brian had said he would meet her at Pearson Airport and take her home with him overnight to break the long journey. She would be happy to see him again. They had much to discuss.

One last evening; on the balcony with a view that was never disappointing. She found a bottle of red with enough left to fill a glass and wrapped her travel coat around her shoulders so she could withstand the cooler sunset breezes until the very last ruddy light had left the sky.

Seagulls flew upward from the tall church tower and circled the town calling their plaintive cries to each other as they searched for another perch. She watched their flight, like a drifting white cloud, and listened to their calls.

Perhaps it was her imagination, but Valerie thought she could hear, 'Haste Ye Back!' in their lonely pleas.

She whispered to the gulls, the mountains, the rivers and the towns; those the women had seen together and others as yet unexplored, "I will come back! If God spares me, I will."

THE END

Now read the sequel! Seven Days *Back* follows the women's stories when they return home and face the reactions of the men in their lives.

The week in the Lake District apartment is over. Valerie, Sandra, Corinne and Zoe have shared secret parts of their lives but now they all return home. There are men in their lives who must now adjust to changes they are not expecting.

www.ruthhay.com

Made in the USA
Lexington, KY
18 October 2016